His Last CHRISTMAS Gift

DEBRA BORCHERT

LE VIN
PRESS

Cover design by Lynn Andreozzi
Book designed and typeset by Elaine Aucoin Schroller

Published by Le Vin Press, Bellevue, WA, U.S.A.

Year of Publication 2025
Library of Congress Control Number: 2025917977

ISBN: 979-8-9899931-3-0 (Ebook)
ISBN: 979-8-9899931-4-7 (Trade paperback)
ISBN: 979-8-9899931-5-4 (Audiobook)

First Edition

Human Authored™ Reg #: 5619452
https://authorsguild.org/human

The Château de Verzat, Award-Winning Series
Her Own Legacy
Her Own Revolution
Her Own War
&

Soups of Château de Verzat:
A Literary Cookbook & Culinary Tribute
to the French Revolution

This Book is Dedicated to Mary & Tom

In Loving Memory of their Beloved Claire

Chapter 1

This was the day Claire had been working toward for twenty-three years. Today she would prove her design worked and would save thousands, no, hundreds of thousands of lives. And she and her boss and Aqua-Line Swimwear would make millions on the patent.

Claire extracted the prototype from the safe in her office. She held out the turquoise and lime-green spandex bathing suit that she'd designed and sewn by hand herself. The slip of fabric wouldn't cover one of her thighs.

Alisha, the fitting model, whose long, shapeless legs reminded Claire of a flamingo's, crossed her arms over her breasts. "What's that contraption?"

"A life preserver." Claire shook out the one-piece suit with trembling hands. Rick had found flaws in all her previous prototypes and shot down every one of them. But he would not find even one tiny glitch in this design. It was perfect. "Just put it on as if it were any other swimsuit. Rick's going to love it. It'll be the best-selling maillot of next season."

With eyebrows lifted in what Claire figured was skepticism, Alisha pulled the Spandex up over her flat hips, nonexistent tummy, and small breasts, then slid her arms under the shoulder straps. Lime-green ruffles draped her biceps. She leaned over, jiggling her breasts into the bra cups, smoothed the straps and stood tall. "It's loose around the bust."

"It's not hooked, yet." Claire fastened the strap in the back and looked out of the door adjacent to the reception area, searching for her boss. She called out to his assistant, "Eleanore, please tell Rick we're ready."

Alisha pulled the fabric. "Still loose around the bust."

"It won't be. Feel this button?" Claire guided Alisha's thumb to the ON button that was sewn into the shoulder strap. "When Rick gets here and I say, 'Go,' press the button. Got it?"

"This puffy thing?"

"Right."

Alisha nodded just as Rick entered Claire's studio. Alisha gave him her dazzling smile, rested her hands on her hips, pushed out her pelvis, and turned on her five-inch heels, snapping her head around making her long black curls whip around her neck. She was a flirt but also a perfect fitting model. Claire gripped her hands like she was praying for her life.

Stroking his graying beard, Rick circled Alisha, examining the suit. He flicked a hand. "Baggy and boring."

"It won't be." Claire pinched her thumb and forefinger. "Go!"

Alisha tilted her head.

"Go ahead. Press the button," Claire urged.

A whooshing sounded as Alisha pressed the strap. Air pumped into the ruffles at the top of her arms, and they puffed out, like a child's water wings. A rubber tube, inserted in the lime green strap circling her chest, inflated like a bicycle tire. Alisha's breasts rose against the plunging neckline, giving her flat chest lovely cleavage. Smiling, Alisha twisted to the right and left before the full-length mirror as her bosom seemed to enhance itself.

Rick's eyebrows popped up. "What the—"

"I've done it. This suit has a built-in life preserver," Claire cried. But then she noticed Alisha's bust continued to enhance.

That was enough inflation to give him the idea. "Okay, release the button," commanded Claire.

Alisha let go of the button. The sound grew louder as her breasts began to bulge over the neckline.

Claire stepped closer. "Release the button."

"I did!"

The tube continued inflating. Claire grabbed the strap and clamped her fingers on the button, pinching it hard.

Alisha pulled the Spandex straps. "Get this thing off me."

The whooshing sound wound higher. The tube bulged beyond Alisha's breasts, growing as large as a child's swim ring circling Alisha's chest. The turquoise Spandex stretched, the color fading as it expanded to accommodate the inflating ring. Claire had no idea the tube could stretch to such a size, but it would keep an adult afloat.

It was working!

But it wasn't stopping!

"Help!" Alisha screeched and shoved at the tube, now the size of a motorcycle tire, struggling to push it down to her waist. The tube bulged. She couldn't grip the slippery fabric covering it. "I can't...breathe."

"Get it off her," Rick shouted.

"You trying to kill me?" she cried.

"I'm so sorry." Claire plucked her fabric shears from the cutting table. "Hold still." She grabbed Alisha with one hand to steady her and inserted one of the blades between the swimsuit and her back. She released Alisha and, with both hands, she snipped.

The wheezing sound filled the room as Claire pulled the tubing away from Alisha's chest. "I'm so sorry. Are you okay?"

Alisha gasped for air. "Dizzy." She bent over. Claire guided Alisha to sit on her chair. Examining the deflated ON button, she said, "I paid three thousand dollars for this prototype—it should have worked, damn it."

Rick rushed to Alisha, shouting, "Are you all right?"

Alisha rounded on Claire, ripping the shoulder strap out of her hands. "You crazy bitch!"

"The pump should have stopped. Did you press it completely?"

"With all my might!"

Claire pulled the tube that ran up the suit's shoulder strap. "Here's why it didn't stop: the switch didn't release." She dropped the strap. "You pushed it too hard."

"You *told* me to push it harder." Alisha ripped the tube away.

"I told you to *release* it."

"You're nuts!" She grabbed her robe from the chair, held it to her bosom, and rushed for the door. "You'll hear from my lawyer."

Rick shouted at his assistant, "Eleanor, call a doctor." He caught up to Alisha and put his arm around her shoulder. "Let me help you."

She smacked her hand against his shoulder. "Get out of my way, or I'll sue you, too!"

He stepped back, his arms hanging as Alisha ran through the design studio and into the showroom.

"Wait!" Claire headed after her.

Rick grabbed Claire's arm and dragged her back into her office. "You could have killed her."

"I'm sorry for what happened, but she's not hurt."

"This is your last *invention*." His tone and sour look made her think he'd stepped in dog poo.

"Don't be ridiculous. It wasn't my fault." She pointed at Alisha. "I must take that suit back to the engineer. We're almost there."

Rick dragged his hands down his face. "You're insane."

"I am not. I'm trying to *save* lives." Claire's fingers vibrated with longing to examine the tubing. "Three thousand people drown every year, and that's just Americans!"

Rick stepped close to her. "Every one of the twenty-three years I've employed you, you have created a life-saver swimsuit. Remember the time you spent two-thousand dollars for fabric guaranteed to float? And the cork bra cups that popped out of the suit and floated away? Another grand. How much did you spend on *this* disaster?"

"Uh…" She stepped away from him.

"You've been trying to incorporate a life preserver in swimsuits since you started working here. Now this—trying to disguise it as a *bust enhancer?*" He stepped closer. "Today, you nearly killed a model with your deranged idea." Another step closer. "You're fired. F-I-R-E-D. Fired!" With the courtesy he'd bestow upon a Neiman Marcus buyer, he opened her office door. "And if she sues me, I'll sue you." He scowled. "Now get out!"

"You're just upset. Tomorrow, you'll recognize this patent is brilliant." Claire stood her ground, hands trembling. "I need the prototype."

Rick grabbed her arm. "You have two minutes to leave on your own before I call security."

"There's no need for security. Alisha's not going to steal the suit."

"For you! I'm calling security to get rid of you! Now get out!" He grabbed the phone from Claire's desk.

"But I'm so close. The patent could make you millions. And save thousands of lives. There's just the switch—a tiny problem."

"The problem, and, it is *not* tiny, is with you, Claire. You're a liability. If that model sues me, I'll lose my business."

"She wasn't hurt."

"How the hell do you know? The thing was suffocating her. She couldn't breathe!"

"Just let me take the suit to the engineer—"

He shouted into the phone, "Security fifth floor." He slammed the phone down on the cutting table. "Out." His nostrils flared like a dog on a hunt. "Now."

"You can't be serious. You hired me to invent a swimsuit with a built-in life preserver."

"I hired you to design swimsuits. Period. And now I'm firing you." He swept his arm toward the door. "Out!"

The studio closed around her, plunging her into a feeling like being dragged by an undertow. Numbness seized her arms. The sound of crashing waves filled her mind and dulled her vision. She shook her head and focused on the walls, hung with sketches, fabric swatches, photos. She stopped, stood still. She was in her studio. The waves ebbed.

Why hadn't the switch released? There was plenty of pressure, too much pressure.

"That's it," she shouted. "There was no resistance! If a woman were in the water and pressed the button, the tube would not have inflated without stopping. As the inside pressure equalized from the water pressure outside the tube, the pump would have stopped, and the inflated tube would float the woman. You can only push the button if you're in the water. There was no water pressure to stop inflation."

"Claire."

"What?"

"You must leave now," he whispered. "I need to make sure Alisha's not scarred."

Two security guards walked down the hall toward her.

"Right." Claire stumbled toward her desk, leaned over, and examined the prototype sketch.

"Claire!" Rick shouted.

She blinked.

The two guards appeared at her side. Rick placed her coat and purse in her arms. Then he lifted her tattered sketchbook, the one she'd brought with her on her first day at Aqua-Line, and gently placed it in her arms. "Good luck, Claire."

"I'll wait for the prototype outside the fitting room." She turned and felt the vice-grip of the guards close around her arms.

They walked her to the elevator—open, empty, and waiting—and escorted her inside. A guard hit the lobby button. She turned as the elevator doors shut out her life.

CHAPTER 2

At home, Claire flung herself face down upon the bed, rolled over, and stared at the ceiling as tears ran in rivulets down into her ears. "Oh, David, I've failed at my invention. And I've been fired." She pounded her fists into the mattress. "And I'm broke."

She picked up the framed photo of him holding a rare bottle of wine at a sommelier's dinner—glowing with pride for his ability to identify it in a blind tasting. "I'm so desperate, I'm talking to you, and you've been gone for more than a year. I know you didn't mean to die without a will, but I may lose our house!" She sobbed and cradled the picture.

They'd never talked about death. They'd never dreamed that it would arrive so early in David's life. Claire knew fabrics and design. She didn't know anything about intestate laws, but she was learning. Not fast enough. An image of a *For Sale* sign on her front lawn surrounded by cardboard boxes made her pulse race. Where would she live? How would she live? On what? "I can't fix this. I need you."

After releasing a sob, she dragged herself to the closet as images of the day he passed clouded her vision. As she reached for David's favorite sportscoat, her fingers tingled, like she'd been stung. She shook her hand and pulled it from the hanger.

She snuggled her face into the jacket. "I miss you." She scrunched the fabric and inhaled, searching for his woodsy, lime scent. "I wish you were here to hold me." She slid her arms into the sleeves, wrapped the jacket around her, and fell onto the bed.

As her hands caressed the soft wool, her fingernail struck a stiff edge. She pressed the pocket, making a crinkling sound. She'd not touched this jacket since the day David died, when she'd been far too upset to notice anything in his pockets. Opening the jacket, she ran her fingers along the inside breast pocket and pulled out a photo of a boy of about six or seven years, standing amidst a vineyard. His eyes were David's. His curly brown hair, David's. His dimples on either side of his smile...David's. Her husband's dimples had lured her the first moment he smiled at her, just as this child's dimples were now snagging her aching heart.

She turned the photo over. In handwritten ink were the words: *Our Luca. Last year's vendange. Merci, Sophie.*

David never missed the French grape harvests; whatever vendange it had been, he must have been there. But *our?* Did Sophie mean she and her husband or David?

Luca had David's eyes, hair, and dimples. Could Luca be the son of a long-lost brother of David's? She was grasping for a lifeline with that far-fetched explanation. David was an only child, just like she was.

There had to be an explanation. David would never cheat.

She sat up. Searched the other jacket pockets. Got up and pulled every jacket, sweater, coat, shirt, pair of pants, robe, pajamas, sweatshirt from the closet and searched every single pocket and sock and shoe and pair of boxershorts. Nothing. Not a penny, business card, or matchbook.

She pulled out David's family photo album and thumbed to the page titled, *Second Grade*. She compared David's school picture with Luca's photo. They looked like twins.

Turning on the bedside lamp, she examined Luca's photo. The boy stood next to an elaborately carved wooden sign with the words, *Château Soltner*. The vineyard had to be in France. If it was in America, Sophie would have used the word, "harvest," not "vendange." The soil was chalky white, the grapes green, the grape leaves yellow and red. White wines were produced there, wherever *there* was.

Dread slid down and sat in the pit of her stomach like wine sediment at the bottom of a bottle. She hadn't been in David's office since she closed the door after the paramedics removed his body. How long had he possessed the photo?

The child was now a year older. Why hadn't Sophie called David or sent him a letter? The image of a pile of unopened mail puddled in her mind. She'd opened all the bills, statements, tax documents, and anything else that appeared official and trashed the rest. But nothing had arrived for David in the past six months.

The doorbell rang.

She groaned. Not now. Not tomorrow. Not ever. She would not answer. It was probably some missionaries, anyway.

A banging on the door echoed in the foyer.

She willed whoever it was to go away. But it could be Holly, the mom next door who had four children. She hoped not, but she couldn't ignore an emergency. She stumbled to the hall and saw a tall, slender, dripping wet Marti peering in through the side window, and she'd spotted Claire. Claire bumped the heel of her hand to her forehead. She'd forgotten their Tuesday lunch.

Just what she needed, her best friend since they were college roommates, from whom she kept nothing.

CHAPTER 3

"Are you all right?" Marti shouted. Her red curls sprayed raindrops as she pummeled the door.

Claire stood rigid as Marti embraced her. "When you didn't show up for lunch, I called your cell and got a weird message saying the number wasn't in service, and then I called your office and they said you didn't work there anymore, and then I called your landline, and it's now a septic tank removal service!"

"Crap."

"Exactly. Why don't you have a landline?"

"I never used it, and I'm trying to save money."

"What's going on?" Marti backed away. Her eyebrows scrunched together. "Why're you wearing David's jacket?"

"David has...had a son." Claire hadn't dared say it aloud, but she'd said it. Her heart felt like a rock, its weight weakening her knees.

Marti hung up her raincoat and wrapped her arm around Claire's waist. "We need a drink." She pulled Claire to the couch, sat her down, and handed her a tissue. "White okay, or does this call for bourbon?" She headed for the kitchen.

"White," whimpered Claire. "Bring the bottle."

"Why is there no food in the fridge, except for cheese and olives?"

"I've been working late at the office."

"Uh huh." Marti handed her a glass of Sauvignon Blanc and set down napkins and a plate of cheese and olives. "Houndstooth is definitely not your color. Why do you think David had a son?" She sat next to her.

Claire handed her the photo.

"Jeesh, he's the spitting image of David." She sipped her wine. "A doppelganger?"

"Too young."

She flipped the photo and read the back. "*Our* Luca?" Marti's sparkling brown eyes bored into Claire. "David wasn't the type to cheat. He adored you. There must be an explanation. Have you looked through his laptop?"

"As confirmation that my husband had an affair?" Claire's hand shook, splashing her wine.

"No." Marti stood. "I'm defending your husband, who I know worshipped you since the day he followed us all over Paris until I left you for five seconds, and he spilled lemonade all over you and fell in love with you." She grabbed a napkin and wiped up the spill. "Could he have donated sperm, I mean for money, when he was a college student?"

"I suppose. He did attend the University of Strasbourg, but I think he would have mentioned it."

Claire stared at the photo, not at all worn or wrinkled, it looked as if David had touched it once, twice maybe. "He must have been wearing this sportscoat the day he died because I found it hanging on his desk chair."

"Meaning the photo might have been news to him? Might that have caused his heart attack?"

"If it was news to him, maybe. But the coroner and David's doctor confirmed he had Sitosterolemia which caused the heart attack. But if it was news to him, the shock could cause a weakened heart to stop, I guess?" She shook her head. "You're the doctor. What do you think?"

"I'm a GP. I'd send you to a cardiologist."

Claire sighed. "When he traveled to France twice a year to buy wines for his clients, he always asked me to accompany him. Every year he tried to convince me. 'We can relive our honeymoon. Remember the fun we had browsing the Christmas markets in Alsace? Let's do it again.' I never went with him." A burbling ran through her stomach. "I was and still am driven by my quest of patenting a life-saving swimsuit. Which seems silly as I say it. Why didn't I *really* want to return to France?" Her vision blurred as if a fog wrapped around her.

"Earth to Claire." Marti put her hands on her hips. "I asked, have you searched his laptop?"

"Rick fired me." She shook her head to clear her mind.

"A week before Christmas? He can't do that." Marti blew out a breath that lifted her bangs. "You've been with that company for more than twenty years. Why?"

"My invention backfired, and the model accused me of trying to kill her, and she ran out of my office, screaming. She threatened to sue." Claire jolted to her feet, trying to see above the fog swirling around her. "I have to call the engineer and order a new prototype."

"Stop it. The model makes a living with her body. If your invention so much as scratched her, she could sue you for lost wages."

"I think she was scared, and I don't blame her, but I don't think she was hurt, at least I hope not."

"Oh Claire. You've become obsessed with this invention."

"You're right. I'm sorry." She pulled David's jacket tighter around her. "I should have gone with him."

"Want to give me a clue about what you're referring to?"

Claire collapsed back onto the couch. "I always told David I couldn't get time away, but really I wasn't ready to start a family."

"Don't you think he knew that?"

"Did he?"

"He constantly joked about how your life-saving swimsuit project was no safety feature for your marriage."

"Do you think he was unhappy?"

Marti headed for the kitchen. "I think he was lonely and missing you."

So was I, thought Claire, but that was my own fault.

Marti put two bottles of mineral water on the coffee table, grabbed Claire's hand, and pulled her to her feet. "Let's search his laptop."

Claire yanked her hand back. "No."

"Why not?"

A numbness in her arms traveled up Claire's shoulders.

"Well, I'm going to try. You stay here and drink." Marti turned toward David's office.

"No, don't!" Claire cried.

"Stop stalling and find out who that child is."

Claire's mouth opened again, but no words came.

"What are you afraid of?"

Claire sucked in her bottom lip. A wave of, she didn't know what, rose in her. She wiped her face and forced words out of an ugly, dark place deep within her. "What if he did have an affair? Then my marriage was all a lie."

Marti sat on the couch and held Claire's hand.

Like trying to pull herself free from an undertow, Claire gripped the edge of the coffee table. "Until that photo, I never acknowledged my obsession as an excuse. I guess I could have gotten time off, but I didn't really want to go to France."

Marti rubbed her eyes. "Oh, Claire," she whispered, "why?"

Why hadn't she? A roaring of water, like she was standing under a waterfall, filled her mind. She covered her ears to stop the sound, but it blared. "Not for my career, which was what I thought and David thought. But..." She looked up at her dearest friend. "I told him I wasn't ready to have children."

"Why?" Her tone was gentle, soothing.

"I didn't know why at the time." Claire rubbed her eyes. "I don't know how to be a mother. I didn't have a good role model. My mother shipped me off to a convent boarding school soon after I learned to walk. I don't know anything about raising a child, other than I know how *not* to do it."

Claire squeezed her eyes, shutting out the image of another woman in her husband's arms. "Our marriage was based on my lies."

"Lies, plural? What else did you lie about?"

Claire bristled. "You my shrink now?"

"No. I only shrink my teenage patients. I'm your friend, and I want to help you. You seem to be forgetting that David loved—"

"And adored me." Claire leaned back into the couch pillows. "When we were getting to know one another, we were hiking in the Alps. David asked the normal family questions, but I remember getting very testy. I didn't want to think about my mother. I told him I hardly knew her and didn't remember her ever hugging me. We hiked along a river, and came to a waterfall, and I freaked out—"

"Wait, you don't like the water. You won't take a ferry. You were surprised the waterfall frightened you?"

"I don't know. I felt disoriented. I shut down, grew quiet and moody. David didn't raise the question again. And I certainly wasn't going to. I guess I was afraid if I went back to France for a romantic second honeymoon, he'd convince me to start a family, and I just couldn't risk that."

"So, you were afraid to be a mom?"

Her vision blurred. "I...I don't know. I never thought about it. I was always just so against becoming a mother, I didn't question why. But, I guess I was." She shook her head, trying to focus.

"And you never discussed your fear with him? Being afraid you won't be a good mother is a pretty big fear. You could have talked to me."

"You might have convinced me, too. I didn't want to be convinced." Claire stood and picked up the framed photo of David and herself on their wedding day. "I don't think I was aware of being afraid while David was alive. I've only just admitted it to myself...and you."

"If Luca is David's son, he also lied."

Longing and regret stewed in Claire's stomach. "That doesn't excuse my lying."

"No. It means we're all human."

Cradling the photo, Claire sank back onto the couch and stared at the ceiling.

"What happened to your cell phone?"

Claire flung out her arm. "The security guards took it and my laptop when they escorted me out of the building."

"The security guards are a conversation for another time. It's not safe to be without a phone. I'm going to get you one. I'll add a new line to our account. It's only ten dollars a month." Marti stood and grabbed her purse. "In the meantime, logon to David's computer and read his email." She kissed Claire's cheek, grabbed her jacket, and left.

An ache skittered across Claire's heart. Did David know she was *afraid* of having children? Afraid of being a mother?

CHAPTER 4

Dust flurried as Claire opened David's office door and switched on the light. She closed her eyes against the image of him lying on the carpet that haunted her every sleepless night for the past year, three months and ten days. She opened the window, letting in cool, damp air, and flipped open the laptop.

As the computer bleeped warnings about updates, she mindlessly clicked the little install boxes. On the bookshelf stood a framed photo so covered in dust, the image appeared as a shadow. She wiped her fingers across the glass and uncovered the photo of Marti and her hugging each other before the Eiffel Tower. They'd backpacked around Europe the summer they'd graduated. David had taken the photo the day Claire met him. The heat of that afternoon washed over her.

Claire and Marti stood drooping in an August heatwave outside Au Printemps's window. They drooled over the mannequins sporting the height of fall fashion.

Marti swiped at the sweat running down her face. "Look at that beautiful plaid wool suit. And the cuffs and patch pockets are suede. It's magnifique! Could you make that for me?"

"I could, but we couldn't afford the wool, never mind the suede." Claire peered closer. "The tailoring is impeccable. That's hand-stitching along the lapels and those are hand-sewn buttonholes. You'd never see that in the States."

After catching a glimpse of their reflections, Claire pressed her sweaty forehead against the glass. "We look like a couple of beached mermaids, only that's not sea water dripping down our necks."

Marti laughed. "Now we know why every French woman flees Paris in August. How can the poor clerks stand working in there? There's not enough air conditioning in the world to cool that place."

A boisterous swarm of teens—who else but Americans would wear Spice Girls T-shirts, cut-off jeans, and platform sneakers in the city of fashion—entered the store. "How do those tourists stand it?" Claire slid the pink gingham triangle scarf from her head and wiped it across her face. Okay it wasn't Parisian style, but it was retro and smaller to pack than a floppy-brimmed sun hat. She had sewn triangle scarves for all the girls in her class at the convent because every one of them was in love with '60s fashion, and, with her scarves, they always had something handy to put on their heads for mass.

Marti took her elbow and pointed. "Let's find a café with a view of the Eiffel Tower and drink our weight in la citronnade. It's one of the things I can pronounce."

They headed west along the Seine. Ducking under an awning, weaving through crowded tables, and storing their backpacks under the tiny round table, they collapsed onto the rattan chairs. Marti examined the woven wicker of her chair. "I want a pair of these and a marble topped bistro table in my kitchen. Such a classic design."

"And it will always remind you of Paris." Claire plucked up le Menu and fanned herself. Hopefully your kitchen will be cooler."

"There's something I've been wanting to tell you."

"You've met someone."

They both laughed so loudly other diners scowled.

"I think I'm a bit punchy from the heat, you too?" Claire asked.

"Seriously. I'm not going to look for an interior design job when we get back to New York."

Claire stopped fanning herself and stared at her dearest friend in the world. They'd been roommates since their first day at college. Would they no longer live together? "Okay...you're not joining the circus are you?"

"I want to be a doctor."

"That *is* a circus." Claire dropped the menu. "How're you going to do that?"

"I applied to NYU for a master's pre-med program because I need to take a bunch of chemistry and biology courses. That's the first step." Marti gazed at something behind Claire, then looked back.

"But you love interior design. You love color and fabrics and wallpaper, and furnishings—" Claire patted the arms of her chair.

"I do. It's fun, but it's not fulfilling. I want to help people. I can decorate my own home and my parents' and yours. I don't know, maybe I can help people redesign their health."

"Wow. That's a huge shift. Why didn't you tell me?" Claire battled the feeling of being left out with her happiness for Marti's decision.

"The idea gnawed at me throughout our last year, but I figured I'd focus on finishing my undergrad degree and at least have that under my belt."

"Maybe we should order Champagne. When do you hear back from NYU?"

"I was accepted!"

"How could you not tell me? Congratulations!" Claire slapped the table. "How did you keep that a secret? We're definitely ordering Champagne."

The waiter, tall, bored, not sweating somehow, stood holding a round tray at shoulder height. "Oui?"

"Let's save the Champagne for tonight, okay?" Marti asked.

Claire nodded and Marti ordered two lemonades. "Let's pray for ice. I told the waiter, 'avec la glace,' but I don't know if I asked for ice or ice cream."

"Either will be cold." Claire squeezed Marti's hand. "I'm so happy for you. Why didn't you tell me?"

"I didn't want to jinx it. I applied for a scholarship and a student loan. While you were still snoozing this morning, I called my folks, and they told me I got both."

"Lots of Champagne tonight. How are your parents taking it?"

She ran her fingers through her damp red curls. "They're thrilled. But even after the scholarship, they're not happy about the tuition, and they don't want me to take out a loan, but I can if I need to. I'll have to get a parttime job."

Claire leaned toward her. "We're still going to be roommates, right?"

"You know I can't live without you."

She relaxed against her chairback. "At least we have reasonable rent, and they can't raise it much thanks to rent stabilization. You could get a weekend job with a designer."

Cutting her eyes to a neighboring table, Marti lowered her voice. "Don't look now, but I think you have an admirer. He's alone and can't pry his eyes off you. Just behind you, to your left, madras plaid shirt."

"Madras? That's as retro as my gingham. At least we have something in common." Claire nonchalantly turned her head and caught a glimpse of a strikingly handsome man. She faced Marti and mouthed, *Wow*! Wrapping the pink triangle around her unwashed hair and tying it at the back of her neck, she prayed the room they got that night would have a shower, even if it was down the hall. "I hope my deodorant's working."

"I don't think he'll notice."

The waiter placed a small dish of olives and two glasses of lemonade on the table. One ice cube bobbed in each drink.

"Ice—the size of a Chicklet—but it's ice." Marti scooped up her glass and rolled it against her cheek. "I'm thinking of our literature class and how *Dante's Inferno* has taken on new meaning. I think I could write a better essay about Hell after surviving this sauna."

Claire laughed. "Do you think we should head north or maybe to the coast for the sea breezes? Back to England for the rain? Maybe the madras guy has a recommendation?"

"I think I should find the ladies' room." Marti got up, nodded to the admirer, like she was in cahoots with him, and walked inside the café.

Claire popped an olive in her mouth. What was Marti up to? Claire dreaded returning to New York, but where else would she find a design job? Her mother had left her enough money for college, but she needed to make her own living now.

She rested her elbows on the table and chose another olive. Something hit the table, causing it to skid away from her. A large hand grabbed it, dragging it back, but it tilted and the glasses toppled. A wave of lemonade splashed across the table and dripped onto her skirt. She gasped.

"Je m'excuse! Désolé." A male voice boomed. "Désolé." A man grabbed a napkin from a nearby table, spewing French as he mopped up the liquid. More French tumbled from him as he mopped and grimaced.

He was the madras-wearing admirer. Had he spilled the drinks on purpose?

The lemonade was more sticky than cool, and it was congealing in the heat. She ripped off her triangle scarf and sopped up the liquid before it drenched her backpack. Her skirt was the last clean thing she had.

"Je m'excuse. Désolé!" He continued spouting French like a whale clearing its blowhole.

She suspected the admirer was asking forgiveness, but his words floated over her. "I...I don't speak French." The word for sorry she knew. She'd used it enough. "Désolée."

"Ah, you are American." His brown eyes danced with mischief as he smiled at her. "Me too. I was trying to protect my camera, I lost the lens cap, and instead of catching it, I bumped your table, and as I tried to right it, I tipped it, and spilled your drinks and really made a mess of things, didn't I? I've ruined your beautiful skirt. You're so fashionably dressed—I thought you were a Parisian. I'll pay to have it cleaned. Please forgive me."

"It's okay. Not a big deal."

"I'm sure a skirt like that is very expensive. I insist."

"Really, I sewed this skirt myself. It didn't cost that much, and I can handwash it." She wrung out the triangle scarf. "In this heat it will dry in seconds."

"You're a very talented designer and a good sport. Still, I'm so sorry. Let me order two more drinks. Is that lemonade? Or do you wish a Kir Royale?"

Her mouth opened and closed but words stuck in her throat as her heart thumped. She was so attracted to his muscled arms, she couldn't get her brain or her mouth to work.

He dragged an empty chair toward her table. "May I join you?" Without waiting for her reply, he slid his chair over next to hers, called the waiter and, from what she could figure out, ordered two more lemonades. She hoped he was paying.

Despite the stickiness, the liquid drying on her skin was at least cooling. Or was her skin heating up from the man's closeness and evaporating the liquid?

"I'm David." He extended his hand and smiled so broadly the two dimples on either side of his mouth dazzled her. He was so warm, friendly...handsome. His eyes were kind and trustworthy. Was he a mirage? A thief? They'd been warned about thieves. She tightened her grasp on her purse strap.

"Your name is..." He pointed.

"Oh, sorry. Um...I'm Claire." She put out her hand. He brought it to his lips and kissed it ever so tenderly. A chill ran through her.

"You're from the States?" He popped an olive in his mouth. "Ah! Picholines, my favorite. Do you like them?"

She nodded, like Scarecrow without a brain, for all she wanted to do was place her hand on his chest, directly above his heart, and feel it beating. What was she thinking? Before they'd left the States, the papers were filled with news of a "date rape drug." She'd keep an eye on her lemonade. She was relieved he was doing all the talking.

"I'm from Boston, but I graduated University in Strasbourg, and I've been traveling for the past year. You?"

"I?" She peeled her skirt from her thighs, shaking out the lemonade.

"I think you've only been here a month, maybe two?

"Uh, huh."

"And you just graduated from college?"

He was a mind reader. "Yes, Pratt Institute."

"Ah, you're here for the fashion!" He struck a model's pose, his arm up, wrist bent, making his fingers look like they belonged to a ballerina, and gazed down his nose as he pursed his lips and batted his eyelashes.

She burst out laughing, realizing she felt as comfortable with him as she did with Marti. She knew she should ask questions of him to get to know him better, but all she could do right then was enjoy him. Or was he just trying to get her into bed? She'd tell Marti never to leave them alone. Where was she anyway? She was probably spying, giving this man all the time he needed to charm her.

Despite her determination to be cautious, she drank him in like a chilled glass of Chablis. His humor and laughter were intoxicating. She could sit across the table from this man every day of her life and never tire of him. Oh, snap—what was she thinking?

Marti returned. "What'd I miss?"

Claire wanted to say, *just my falling in love with a complete stranger*, but resisted. That was the craziest thought she'd had in her lifetime. Her confession could wait until dinner and Champagne.

Marti pointed. "And you are?"

"I'm David." He stood and pulled out Marti's chair. "Enchanté."

"Marti." She sat and looked from Claire to him and back to Claire. Marti smiled conspiratorially, as if David and she had arranged this meeting.

The waiter arrived with three flutes sparkling with dark pink liquid at the bottom of the glass and Champagne floating in a layer above.

"Kir Royale. I hope you like them. I spilled your lemonades on Claire, and I feel I must make up for my calamity. Please forgive my intrusion." He lifted his glass. "The French say, 'Santé.' To your health."

Claire clinked her glass to his and then to Marti's. "Congratulations on your new endeavor as a doctor," she whispered.

After one sip Claire thought she might forgive David anything. "Delicious!"

She might forgive David anything? She plucked up a tissue and wiped the dust from the silver frame. The laptop dinged, jarring her. Hugging the photo, she sat down. The welcome login screen finally appeared. She and David shared their passwords, but she had enough trouble remembering her own, much less his. She typed in his email address and what she thought might be the password he always used, the unpronounceable town where they were married and that year: *Riquewihr1997*.

The screen blinked as thousands of emails scrolled. Pages upon pages of messages from Amazon and credit card companies and investment opportunities in third-world countries.

Once she'd deleted the junk, only three remained, all from David's former boss, asking why he wasn't answering his phone on the day David died. The memory of that moment sliced through her as clean and sharp as the moment she'd discovered him.

She searched his Sent Mail folder for any mention of Luca, Sophie, and Soltner. Nothing.

She put her face in her hands and didn't fight the tears. The worst had happened. Why was she scared now?

She sat up. Because if David cheated on her, she'd lost him long before he died.

She didn't want to believe David had been unfaithful, but if he was, she would have to face losing the life she thought they'd shared and lose him all over again. She didn't think she could live with losing him twice.

Who was this woman, Sophie? Surely she knew David was married. Didn't she? Had Claire the courage to accept the truth? The only person who knew that truth was Sophie.

She googled Sophie Soltner, Luca Soltner, and Château Soltner. No website, no phone number, no email address, no physical address, just a brief description of the vineyard, a list of its varietals, and a map locating the château outside Colmar in the Alsace region of France.

She blew out a slow hot breath. David, too, had lied. He had a son. A son who didn't know his father. A son who was probably missing his father.

She'd never met her father, but she did have a vague memory of a dark-haired man with a beard, cuddling her. Was he her father? *Unknown* appeared in the line for father on her birth certificate. All the while she was at the convent, there was nothing to remind her that she didn't have a father, so she didn't have anything to compare her single-parent existence to.

She picked up the photo. Luca had David's dimples. Did he have David's sense of humor and laugh?

Something in her stomach twisted. Her mouth went dry. Could Luca have inherited David's heart condition?

David never knew he had Sitosterolemia—he had no symptoms of heart disease, had a healthy diet, and exercised—yet he died at fifty of a heart attack. When the coroner declared the cause of death a heart attack, Claire demanded more tests be done as David had low cholesterol and no health issues. A DNA test revealed mutations in two genes, confirming David had inherited Sitosterolemia. David's doctor patiently explained the test results and details of his cause of death with compassion. She remembered thinking it was good that they hadn't had children as David's condition was hereditary. Having been in shock at the time, she didn't remember all the facts.

She typed Sitosterolemia in the search bar. As she read page after page filled with terrifying statistics, the room darkened and closed around her. The condition was the leading cause of sudden, heart-related deaths in young people, and their parents were never aware anything was wrong. She imagined being a mother whose son or daughter died as a child. She'd be devastated, as would any mother.

But early death was preventable with diet and medication—if the condition was diagnosed, which was rare as even doctors were not familiar with Sitosterolemia.

She had to notify Sophie. Luca had to be tested.

Caressing the photo of Luca, she promised herself she'd figure out how he became David's son later. She would not let Luca die young.

She searched for cheap flights to Paris.

CHAPTER 5

Claire placed her rain shoes, toiletry kit, and makeup clutch at the bottom of her roller bag. Atop them she folded two pairs of slacks, three turtlenecks, a nightgown, socks and underwear. As she rolled the bag to the living room, the doorbell rang. The Uber driver wasn't supposed to arrive for another hour.

A dripping Marti, clutching a hot pink and white bag, stood at the door. She grinned. "Phone delivery."

Claire took her coat and hung it in the hallway. "Thank you."

"Just enter your account email address and password, and all your emails and contacts should automatically download. Do it before I leave for the clinic."

Claire opened the bag and sat on the couch.

"Going somewhere, like France?"

"Yep. France."

"No, no, no, no, no. I was kidding. Are you out of your mind?"

"I'm more *in* my mind than I have been since David died."

Marti sat next to her and gripped her hands. "Isn't flying to France grotesquely expensive? Your attorney told you

David's estate won't be out of the courts until after January."

"I'm flying stand-by. With the bad weather, there should be a seat available because of missed connecting flights." Claire turned the phone toward Marti. "It works. You're a genius."

"Forget the phone. You found Sophie?"

"No."

"Talk to me."

"I only know that the Soltner vineyard is in Alsace, near Colmar." Claire brought her shoulders to her ears and released them with a sigh. "I spent most of last night collecting the latest information on Sitosterolemia." She pointed to the nine-by-twelve envelope sitting on the coffee table.

Marti picked up the packet. "There's two inches of paper there. Ever hear of a flash drive?"

"I'm not taking a laptop, and I want to read through the information to see if there've been any advances in cures while I'm on the plane. David was a carrier of the gene that causes it. That means Luca has a fifty percent chance of inheriting it. I hope Sophie speaks English."

Marti held Claire's hand. "You know that meeting Sophie may bring to light things you may not want to know about David?"

She nodded. "In my heart I believe David was faithful to me, but as you pointed out, he might not have been, and if so, I will have to live with that." The thought sucked the air from her lungs. "But children die of heart attacks caused by Sitosterolemia, some as young as five-years-old, and, like David, they may not exhibit any symptoms."

"Why not wait until after the holidays, when it'll be easier on you? I could even come with you."

"If something happened to Luca, knowing I could have prevented it, I would never forgive myself. It would be like losing David all over again."

Marti's smile was sad. "I think I understand. You're very brave—and thoughtful."

Claire shrugged. "I'm desperate. I'll do everything in my power to protect Luca whether he is or isn't David's son."

"You might be desperate, but it requires courage to take action. You're going on a huge journey, and I don't mean by plane, I mean an emotional journey."

"I wish you could come with me."

"The holidays are the most difficult time of the year for many people and therefore my busiest. I can't abandon my patients, especially without any notice. You have a phone now, and you can call me anytime. And I want you to send me photos. Promise?"

Claire nodded. "Thank you for respecting my decision."

"Like I could stop you?"

"You're supporting me, and that means the world to me."

I'll always support you. Just be back in time for Christmas. We can't celebrate without you."

Claire hugged her. "I love you."

"I love you, too. Call me when you get to the airport. I'm sure I'll have thought of other things I need to warn you about."

Claire laughed, walked Marti to the door, and held out her coat.

"Do you have a spare umbrella?"

Claire pulled one out of the closet.

"Be careful!" Marti hugged her. "Text me the name of your hotel and flight number."

"I will." Claire stared at her dearest friend's back. She'd be careful, but how would she stop worrying about what she might learn about her husband?

CHAPTER 6

A kind flight attendant helped Claire download a transportation app and book her ticket to Colmar on a train that departed right from the Paris Charles de Gaulle airport. After buying coffee and a croissant, Claire found her window seat, put her coffee cup on the tray table, and heaved her roller bag up onto the rack above.

She sat and bit into the croissant—the shattering of its flakey pastry, the flurry of crumbs falling into her cupped hand, the chewy, silky interior dough on her tongue, the addictive butter, creamy and salty—her senses took her back to Sunday mornings in bed with David, café au lait, and croissants. They'd called them love breakfasts because all that delicious decadence led to lovemaking. With their active sex life, it was a wonder she didn't become pregnant, but she'd used birth control, and that worked anywhere you happened to be. Why had she been so resistant to returning to France with him?

Something was bugging her. When was the last time David asked her to join him? The memory of that night swamped her.

The house was so dark, Claire didn't think David was

home. She hoped they wouldn't repeat their yearly arguments about starting a family again. When she unlocked the door, the aroma of steak au poivre lured her to the kitchen where she knew she'd find her husband. Candles perched on shelves, along the top of the refrigerator, the counters, and windowsills. A battered silver antique candelabrum sporting eight flickering candles sat on the bistro table. Charles Aznavour sang *Bon anniversaire* over the speakers. A lemon tarte, her favorite, sat on the counter surrounded by raspberries and candles.

"Bonsoir." David slid his arms around her and kissed her deeply.

She luxuriated in his passion. "That welcome makes me think we should have anniversaries more often, like every day."

"We'll start tomorrow." He released her and handed her a Kir Royale. "To the happiest fifteen years of my life, and the four months it took me to convince you to marry me."

"And to the happiest fifteen years and four months of my life. I'm so glad you spilled lemonade all over me. Thank you."

"I'll do it again, any time." He winked.

She ran to the hall closet for his gift, returned, and placed the box on the counter. "Voila. Bon anniversaire. I've learned a few more French words over the past fifteen years thanks to you."

His dimples deepened as he tore open the wrapping paper. "Wow. How did you know I wanted this lens? And it's a Nikon!"

"Maybe because you complain about not having one." She finished her Kir. "I think I can pronounce dinner too."

He pulled out a chair for her, sat opposite and poured glasses of Château Lafite Rothschild.

"Can we afford this?" she exclaimed.

"This is the bottle I won at the Sommelier Blind Tasting." He brought up his glass. "To you."

She laughed and clinked her glass against his. "And you." Watching his kind, loving eyes, she sipped the dark ruby wine, robust and fruity, rich and smooth as velvet. How had she been so lucky to marry not only a kind man, but also a man who knew wines and how to cook? "Mmm. Black current and truffle."

"I taste a bit of tobacco as well." He handed her an envelope. "Your gift, Madame. And it would be the most wonderful gift to me, if you accept it."

"Hmm. What does that mean?" She held the envelope up to the light. "A Victoria Secret gift certificate?"

Mischief danced in his eyes as he shook his head.

She waved it. "Jewelry?" She sniffed it. "A very flat bottle of perfume?"

She opened the envelope. A tightness encircled her lungs. First-class plane tickets to Paris. "Wow. That's very...romantic and...thoughtful."

David's dimples deepened as his face glowed with pride. "I cleared it with your boss. He approved your vacation time."

Heat rose in her face. "You spoke to Rick without asking me?"

"I wanted it to be a surprise."

"I'd never talk to your boss behind your back." She took a sip of wine, but the richness now tasted tart. "I appreciate your wanting it to be a surprise, but asking Rick was intrusive. And unprofessional." She dropped the tickets on the table. "I'd never talk to your boss, behind your back, period."

He sat back, his shoulders rounding. "I've asked you to accompany me on every trip I've taken to France since we were married there." He rotated his fork making a circle on the white linen tablecloth. "You've always said you couldn't get away. You've declined my invitation twice a year for every year of our marriage, that's thirty times, including tonight. I wanted to make it easy for you to get away, so we could commemorate our marriage."

Her jaw was so tight it throbbed. She took a long drink of wine. "Going away will make my return more stressful. There is no one to take on my responsibilities, and I'll be slammed with work when I get back. I hate working under all that pressure. I don't want to take time off." She balled up her napkin and threw it on the table.

"You'd not be taking time off," he whispered. "You'd be taking time to be with me."

He was hurt, rightfully so. She wanted to be with him—she just didn't want to be controlled by him. Her head pounded. "It's not a good time."

"It'll never be a good time unless you take the time." Hurt rose in his eyes.

She softened her words. "I'll take the time, just not now."

"What are you afraid of?" His tone grew impatient.

"I'm afraid of being overwhelmed by work and losing my job."

"Why would you lose your job? You're Rick's star. He'd never let you go." He poured more wine into her glass.

"How do you know? I'm his only designer. There's no one else who can pick up the slack when I'm not there. Rick said yes to you to be polite, not because he can run his business without me."

"Why don't you want to go to France? We met there, fell in love there, had a wonderful time there, got married there."

Something rock-hard sat in Claire's stomach. Everything he said was true, so true that she knew if she returned to the place they'd fallen in love, he'd sweep her off her feet again, and he'd convince her to start a family, and she'd get pregnant, and she just wasn't ready.

David shook his head and rotated his fork back and forth like a windshield wiper. "The real issue here is you not wanting a family, which you said you wanted."

Her face burned as if his words had slapped her. "We have the same argument every year. And every year you don't listen to me." Maybe he knew her better than she did. That rock sitting in her stomach grew sharp and she hated herself for her words before she said them. "You're bringing up children on our anniversary is not a good way to get them!"

"I am an only child, and I was lonely. I want a family. I would think you'd want children, too."

"I do, just not now."

"It's been fifteen years. How long do you want me to wait?"

"I want a family, I really do, but when the time is right."

"Time is not right or wrong. You're thirty-eight. If we wait much longer, we'll have no time."

"I don't like being forced into anything."

"I didn't force you to love me, I'm not forcing you to want children or a family, I'm not forcing you to go to France. I'm asking you to be with me."

"I know. I love you. But I'm not ready for a vacation in France. And I'm not ready to have children!"

"Are you afraid you can only get pregnant in France? It works the same way here, too, you know."

She poured herself more wine. "You can be very romantic. I can just imagine you in a bubble bath, where you proposed, convincing me the time is right, and I acquiesce. And then I regret my decision because," she slammed her glass on the table, "I'm...not...ready!"

"On our first anniversary I asked you why you were afraid of becoming a mother, which I deeply regret because you left the house and didn't return for two days. I was frantic, so frantic that when you did return, I vowed never to ask you that question again. Until now. Why are you afraid of becoming a mother?"

"I'm sorry I left. I won't do that again." She worried her hands. "I don't know if I fear becoming a mother or if it's because I don't know how to be one, but the thought of becoming a mother totally overwhelms me." She reached out to him, and he backed away. "I'm just not ready. I'm sorry."

He picked up the tickets and his glass of wine. "I don't think you will be ready—ever." He left her and shut himself in his office.

She hadn't thought she would ever grow tired of sitting opposite the table from him—and she wasn't tired of him—but she was tired of the same conversation that accompanied every anniversary. She was tired of feeling pressured. Many career women put off having children, and some chose not to. Marti and Stephen didn't have kids.

She inhaled the aroma of the brandy-peppercorn sauce. It wasn't fair that he'd cooked this delicious dinner and she'd be the only one to eat it. But she wasn't about to call a truce or let the steak go to waste.

She filled her plate and cut a double slice of lemon tarte and appreciated it all with Charles Aznavour as he sung *La Bohème*, about moments of joy, moments of pain.

The train slowly moved out of the station. She jolted at a realization: that night was the last time David had asked her to join him—thirteen years ago. She remembered being relieved he hadn't brought up the family discussion again...and now she wished he had. She wondered if David gave up and decided to have a child without her. If he made a conscious decision to have a child, if he'd thought about it for a while, or maybe he'd been trying with someone else for a few years. Luca was seven or eight years old. Did David even know about Luca when the child was born?

She swallowed back guilt that was more bitter than the coffee. She'd not been honest with her husband. But she'd also not been honest with herself. Marti helped her uncover her fear of becoming a mother. She certainly didn't want to be the cold, critical woman her mother had been. But Claire wasn't cold or critical. Did having a child change her mother?

She wished the coffee had brandy in it, to help wash away the guilt for her procrastination and never giving David children. Which, for the first time in her life, she deeply regretted.

She forced herself to be honest now: her marriage wasn't as perfect as she'd thought. They'd both harbored secrets that prevented a deep intimacy between them. Was getting to know her husband better a part of the reason she flew five thousand miles? And maybe get to know herself, better?

The train stopped in Paris, and hordes of children of all ages, parents, retired couples, backpacking students filled the car. A businessman dressed in a trench coat and plaid scarf sat next to her, placed his briefcase on his lap, and whipped out his phone, keeping it two inches from his face. She took his action as a warning that he was not available for polite conversation. Just as the door dinged a young couple, vibrating with lust, hopped up the steps and into the row opposite Claire.

They laughed heartily as the man tossed their backpacks up on the rack and collapsed into his seat. The train jolted forward. The woman giggled and snuggled into him. He caressed her hair, kissing her forehead.

Their intimacy made Claire turn to look out the window, but the station was dark, and the glass reflected her face, lined with anxiety, staring back at her. She and David had been exactly like that couple, full of love and nonsense. She closed her eyes and saw David sitting in a bubble-filled bathtub opposite her, placing a ring on her finger, asking her to marry him. Three days later, they'd stood amongst a brace of candles at a ceremony on the altar of a tiny chapel surrounded by snow-laden fir trees on Christmas Eve.

With a whoosh and the blare of the train's horn, the train sped through a railyard and beyond the city limits, passing suburban villages. The memories of David's explanations of the village customs, architecture, and crops lulled her into believing he was there, next to her, whispering his love and devotion. She jolted awake, took a gulp of coffee.

Feelings gnawed at her stomach, and she didn't think the sensation had anything to do with food. Was it anger at David if he'd knowingly kept his son a secret from her? Regret for not having been honest with each other? Guilt over not giving David kids. Grief over his death—coated with her sense of betrayal, for no matter how David had a son, he'd not told her, unless he had learned about it the day he died, and he'd not had time to tell her.

A University loomed in the distance. University of Strasbourg was David's alma mater, where he'd earned a sommelier degree. He'd put himself through college, and it was possible Marti could be right, that he'd donated sperm for the money. A torrent of rain splattered the window. Good grief, if he had, she would have to notify all the recipients.

The couple across from her burst into laughter. The woman mock-punched the young man and threw herself back into her seat with a pout.

Claire longed to hide behind a newspaper. Did they print them anymore? She sighed and dug out her phone and searched IVF, Strasbourg. Pages of fertility clinics appeared. She typed, *How long can frozen sperm remain viable for IVF?* The answer, decades, surprised her. She requested, *Is there a limit to the number of children a sperm donor can give rise to,* and learned that every country had their own restrictions. France allowed six families to be recipients, but there was no limitation on the number of siblings. Could David have donated to more than one family? Could Luca have siblings? Her searching was not helping. The information was fueling the gnawing in her stomach.

She would only have to find the service where David donated, if he donated, God, she hoped he'd donated. They could inform the recipients of the hereditary risk. Maybe Sophie would know the name of the service. She should have brought more copies of his medical records.

The woman across from her giggled and spread her quilted coat across her and her lover and kissed him passionately. He reached his hand under the coat and smiled wickedly. The woman let out a groan.

Good God they were going to enjoy heavy petting, if not more, not a foot away from Claire. Really, did they not comprehend privacy? This was an over-the-top public display of affection. If she wanted to watch an X-rated movie, she'd watch TV.

She opened her ticket to check how much longer she had to endure their taunting. Ten minutes. She picked up her cup and *accidentally* spilled its contents on the couple's feet. They bolted out of their seats, sputtering French, no doubt cussing, both glaring at her.

Claire lifted her shoulders, pressed her hand to her cheek, and giggled. "So sorry. Désolée." She shrugged on her coat, grabbed her purse, smiled at the young man, and mimed getting her bag down. He was only too happy to comply. She thanked him and pulled her bag toward the door. At least the couple was a distraction, if not an irritation.

The train slid into the station and Claire dragged her bag out into the snow toward a towering Christmas tree decked in blue lights, silver stars, and glittering gold ornaments. She hoped the Uber driver spoke English and the hotel was near.

CHAPTER 7

After creeping along crowded, cobblestoned streets and crossing ancient bridges over canals and a river, the driver stopped. Claire climbed out from the back seat and steadied herself against the car door.

Shutters framed every mullioned window in the half-timbered, five-floored stone château. Thousands of white lights decorated pine boughs wrapped around columns and balconies. Two petite Christmas trees, bedecked with electric candle lights, stood sentry on either side of the entrance, twinkling in welcome.

The front doors had been carved pine when she and David honeymooned in this hotel more than twenty-five years earlier. Otherwise, the establishment was the same, probably since the seventeenth century. The glass doors opened, and a waterfall of French spoken by a dark haired, elegant woman welcomed her into the wood-paneled reception area.

"I am Claire Didier."

Another torrent of French rang like a song.

Claire wished she could remember the French she'd studied, but nothing besides *Bonjour* came to mind. "I'm sorry, I don't speak French."

"Ah. I am so sorry, Madame Didier. As your husband does, I assumed you do as well. Where is Monsieur?" Her kohl-rimmed dark eyes sparkled. "We haven't seen him in more than a year."

This was a small town. Claire didn't think she should pass on this news in case Sophie didn't know and heard it. She'd be terribly shocked. Yet, this woman deserved to know. She'd tell her after she told Sophie. "I'm alone and very tired. If I could please go to my room?"

"Of course. We'll be sure to welcome Monsieur when he arrives. We have his usual room all ready, at his usual discounted rate. Your passport please."

David's discount awakened Claire's curiosity, and she handed over her passport.

"You'll be with us for a week?"

Claire had no idea, but she knew the hotel was in high demand during the Christmas season. "Yes, I think so."

The woman nodded. "I'm Chrissy and will be happy to arrange anything you like. Your luggage is awaiting you. Follow me please."

Claire hesitated. "Can you tell me...do you know the address of the Soltner Vineyard?"

The woman laughed. "Everyone in Colmar knows the Soltner Vineyard. You wish to visit?"

"Tomorrow morning."

"Drivers know it well. Just call the front desk ten minutes before you wish to leave, and we'll arrange for a car to be waiting."

Claire could have kissed her. How was the place known throughout Colmar yet not have a website? She followed

Chrissy up a sweeping, red-carpeted staircase with hearts carved out of the white pine balustrade. She climbed a second flight of steps and walked down a quiet corridor to the last room. She tripped on the thick carpet. Room 22. Their honeymoon suite *and* David's usual room.

Tiredness pulled at her arms and legs. How would she survive the memories?

Just like her last visit, ancient wood beams crossed the white walls and ceiling. Tall, double-paned windows overlooked the courtyard. A comfy couch sat in a side nook. New gray silk drapes hung on either side of the windows and the headboard of the inviting queen-sized bed. A round intimate table for two, wearing a matching floor-length gray silk skirt, stood before the window. Chrissy pulled a corkscrew from her pocket and opened the bottle of white wine chilling in a silver ice bucket sitting on the table next to a platter of cheeses, grapes, and a baguette. Two crystal wine glasses shone in the soft light. Chrissy poured a glass of wine and handed it to her.

Claire inhaled a slightly fruity aroma and sipped a divinely crisp vintage—bright with a hint of sweetness. She remembered the Rieslings and Gewürztraminers they'd tasted when they'd honeymooned here. She found the Rieslings cloyingly sweet, but the Gewürztraminers were a bit peppery, spicy. This wine was dry, more like a Chablis, but not quite as light, with a fruity taste she couldn't quite place.

Chrissy put the heavy, old-fashioned room key on the table. "I'll keep an eye out for Monsieur Didier. Pleasant dreams."

Claire dreaded having to tell the charming woman that David wouldn't be returning. She also knew her dreams would be everything *but* pleasant. She removed the linen napkin wound around the wine bottle and examined the label. Château Soltner, Muscat, Vin D'Alsace. No address or website on it either.

She ripped off a piece of baguette. She never knew David had always reserved the suite in which they'd spent their honeymoon.

She peeked into the bathroom—the same marble soaking tub they'd enjoyed on their wedding night. They'd soaked until the water chilled then ran laughing to the bed and dove under the down comforter. She didn't remember leaving their room for three days.

The realization that he'd been a hopeless romantic hit her, and a yawn of hurt opened in her at the thought of disappointing him by not joining him here. She'd never forgive herself. Had David? The same portrait of Bartholdi standing before his Statue of Liberty hung in the same place on the wall. They had turned it over when they made love, not wanting him to witness their intimacy.

A soft Christmas carol of bells played in the courtyard. She stared beyond the wavy, glass-paned window. A little girl screeched with delight as her father and mother held her hands and lifted her, high enough to see a lit-up Santa and his reindeer atop a café's roof.

Claire shut the drapes on their joy, their laughter, their loving family. She rested her forehead against the smooth fabric. *David, I am so, so sorry I was such an idiot.*

She finished the glass of wine and fell onto the bed, hoping she was jet-lagged enough to sleep. She would learn many things in the morning, and she needed to find the courage and fortitude she didn't possess.

Chapter 8

The taxi sped by rolling hills dusted in snow and valleys covered in rows of grape vines, brown tangly things without color, fruit, or leaves—barren. She massaged the base of her thumb. How would she tell Sophie about David's death? She didn't want Sophie or Luca to witness her grief—but how could she hide it? Grief still gnawed at her heart.

She shook the tension from her fingers. She had to get David's medical records to Sophie so Luca could be tested and live a very long life. If David had been a donor, she would ask Sophie the name of the clinic where he donated, so Claire could give them his medical records, and they could notify other families.

If there were other families who'd received David's donations, would she also want to meet those children?

Trying to calm the brawl in her gut—roiling with anxiety, trepidation, nervousness, despair, an odd sense of hope that David had been a donor, and the terror of him having had an affair—she concentrated on the dazzling stream curving its way down the valley, crystalline ice capping boulders. Frost framing the windows of cottages, snow-dusted pine boughs, smoke curling like ribbons from chimneys. Little wonder the Alsace region claimed to be the Christmas capital of the world.

She had always loved the holiday season. At the sight of a white steeple in the distance, she wondered if she could find the tiny stone church in Riquewihr, where they were married. Or the former mill made into a guest house they stayed in prior to the wedding—where a bat had made his home amongst the eighteenth-century rafters. She laughed, remembering David, holding a towel over his head while snapping another at the poor creature to chase it out the window, all while she cowered under the bed.

She would have to figure out how to say the unpronounceable Riquewihr; David had tried to get her to say it, but was it *RIke-veer? Or REEK-vir?* She had laughed too hard to pay attention.

The taxi turned and climbed a hill to a building surrounded by vineyards. Sunshine glared off an ice-coated stone roof at its pinnacle. Slowly, a butter-colored château with blue shutters and trim appeared beneath the roof. A waist-high, stone-walled well with an ornate pulley system above it stood in the center of a courtyard, surrounded on three sides by the château.

"Voila, Madame." The driver flicked his hand toward the house.

"Please wait."

"Bien."

She took that for an OK and got out. Pine perfumed the crisp air, reminding her of the frigid night breezes that drafted into her dormitory at her Vermont boarding school. She pulled her purse strap onto her shoulder and cautiously stepped onto the icy gravel path and headed to the front door. She forced her lips to smile, but fear shivered through her. Her whole idea of her marriage could come crashing down around her ankles, and on top of that, she had to deliver terrible news and a potentially threatening medical report.

A rustling of bushes and a woofing stopped her, mid-step. A dog the size of a bear bounded, his black and brown curly fur flouncing, his tail vibrating. She reached for the well, but her hand slid on the icy stone wall.

The force of the beast knocked her flat on her back, and the weight of him sitting atop her kept her there. Her chest ached. He slurped her face with his surprisingly soft tongue. He seemed to smile at her. Drool dripped from his chops onto her coat.

"Remy! Vien ici!"

The dog turned, looked at a man, who she took as his master, and whined, as if to say, *But I'm having so much fun.*

The man clapped his hands, and the bear-of-a-dog pressed his paws further into her chest, practically cracking her ribs, before bounding off.

"Madame!" The dog's master knelt at her side speaking French at the speed of light, his tone kind, concerned. "Désolé!"

Sparks circled her vision as she blinked. The man was about her age, salt and pepper hair in need of a good cut and styling, and a matching shaggy moustache. His eyes were bright blue-gray and deep laughter lines curled across his weathered cheeks.

She sucked in air, enabled by the absence of the beast. "I...I don't...parlay French."

"You're American." His tone was accusatory. The laugh lines disappeared as a frown pleated his forehead.

"Is that a crime in France?"

"Non! No, no, no, no, no." He offered his hand. "Are you hurt?"

"I don't think so. Just had the wind knocked out of me." She pushed herself up on her elbows. Pain zagged across her shoulders.

He scrunched his eyes. "The wind?"

"It's an idiom." She patted her chest. "My breath."

He nodded, held her hand, and gripped her arm as he pulled her to her feet.

She welcomed his help, stood, and caught a scent of pine and...bergamot, perhaps?

He gripped his hands in prayer. "Désolé. I mean, sorry. Remy is terribly friendly. He didn't hurt you?"

She shook her head. The dog lay to the side of the path, ears raised in curiosity, nose quivering.

"Bon. How can I help you?"

She swiped at the muddy paw prints and puddle of saliva on her coat. "Is Sophie home?"

Lines gathered across his forehead like storm clouds. "Non."

"When will she return?"

"Who are you?" He crossed his arms.

His eyes drilled into hers, making her take a step back. She was glad she had thought of a story if Sophie had a husband. She had rehearsed this and had it down pat. "We met at a wine event a few years ago, and Sophie told me to visit her when I returned, so, here I am." A nervous laugh escaped.

"You are...?"

She tapped her head. "Sorry, I'm Claire." Her hand shot out, but he stood rigid. "You are?" she asked.

"Where was this *event*?" His lips pressed into a tight line.

He had to be Sophie's husband. Claire would not say anything that would reveal Luca's true father. The man might not know, and, even if David had cheated on her, she couldn't enlighten this man and wreck his marriage. Her fingers shook as she wiped hair from her eyes. "I have a terrible memory. But she sent a photo of Luca with her last Christmas card and invited me to meet him." She smiled, proud of her plan.

The man neared. "You a child-napper?"

"What?" She backed away. "No. Whyever would you say such a thing?"

His eyebrows hooded his eyes. "You Americans think your country is the best, so you think America is the best country for Luca?"

"No. Of course not."

"Go back to America."

"I just wanted to say hello to Sophie and meet Luca." His eyes held fury but why? "Who are you?" she asked.

"None of your business. Get out of here. Leave. Now!"

"You're quite rude, do you know that?"

"Americans are the rudest people on earth," he growled.

If he was Sophie's husband and knew about David, she wouldn't blame him for hating Americans. "I really need to see Sophie. It's very important." Claire pulled her head back. "Would you kindly tell her I stopped by?" She squared her shoulders, dug out the business card from the hotel and held it out.

He pointed at the taxi.

Why was he being so obstinate? Did he know Sophie had been unfaithful? In her heart and mind, Claire had promised David she would deliver his medical records to Sophie—if Luca inherited David's heart condition the child was in extreme danger. She'd flown five-thousand miles, and she wasn't about to give up, but she did need to be cautious. This guy could be an ax murderer. She stood tall, walked to the front door, shoved the card under it, and smiled a fake smile as she returned to the taxi.

She opened the taxi door and turned to the inhospitable, handsome man. "My name is Claire Didier, and I'm staying at L'hôtel la Rivière." She got in the taxi, slid across the seat, and slammed the door. "My hotel, please."

"Oui, Madame." The driver backed away.

Claire stared at Sophie's husband as he clapped his hands, releasing the dog who leaped up and licked the man's face. At least one creature liked the jerk. She couldn't help but feel a bit of compassion for him. He might have been cheated on. Betrayed. But he also was threatened, and protective of Luca.

She failed David once again. She failed at her invention, failed at her job, failed at giving David a family. Now she'd failed to protect his son.

The countryside undulated as they drove, but Claire didn't appreciate it. Tears slid off her jaw as the spires of

Colmar churches appeared in the distance. *I promised I'd get your medical records to your son's mother, David. And I won't leave France until I do.*

CHAPTER 9

Icicles hanging from the roof glittered in the bright sunlight. A steady drip of melting ice pattered like rain. Claire slipped between the drops, entered the hotel, and walked straight to the bar.

A broad-backed woman wearing a white blouse with puffy sleeves, a dirndl skirt, and embroidered apron stood at the bar drying glasses. "Bonjour Madame Didier." Her phrase sounded like a robin's song.

"Bonjour, Madame. You not only attend the front desk and arrange taxis but also tend bar?"

"I do everything! My husband and I own the place." She laughed as she dragged her bar rag across her forehead. "What will you take?"

Claire pulled out a stool and sat at the blond-wood bar facing shelves of earthenware pitchers. "Is it too early for a glass of wine?"

"Not in Alsace." The woman picked up one of the smallest pitchers. "Un petit pichet?"

Removing her coat, Claire nodded.

"Red or white?"

Claire put up her hand. "Do you have any Soltner wines?"

The woman cocked her eyebrow. "What do you know of Château Soltner?"

Her response was rather challenging, but this woman spoke English, and if Claire wanted information, she'd have to give it. "I only know my husband frequented the cave, and I believe he bought their wines for distribution in America."

"I know your husband well." She extended her hand. "I am Justine."

Claire shook her hand. "Claire."

Justine nodded slowly. "Many evenings, your husband sat right where you are sitting now and told me of his tastings at all the vineyards. Is he tasting at a vineyard now? We've missed him over the past year."

Heat rose into Claire's face, and she knew she was blushing with shame. She ought to tell this woman, but not before she told Sophie. "He's traveling."

Justine's grip on the pitcher tightened. "I'm glad you finally joined him. He often spoke of you and promised one day you'd come along."

A tingling ran down Claire's back, and she leaned into the chair hoping to dull it. This woman was a touch judgmental. "David must have told you I traveled to China and India for business. The last thing I wanted to do for vacation was to get on another plane."

She tsked. "For a woman who was married in Riquewihr and spent her honeymoon in this very hotel, you are not very...*romantique*."

Definitely judgmental. How much had David told this woman? Had he spoken of his son? Regardless of the pain of that truth, she needed to learn it. "I guess not. Did...does David like Soltner wines?"

"Madame, everyone loves Soltner wines." She pulled a bottle from the refrigerator below the bar. "But..." she tilted her head and pushed out her lower lip. "We shall see." She poured white wine into the pitcher. "This is a Muscat, very rare for this region, from Soltner. Your husband recommended it, and I now serve it here."

Claire poured a bit of the same wine she'd had the night before into a glass and sipped, pretending she'd never tasted it. "Lively, aromatic, crisp. It's great."

"Of course. Your husband is a wine connoisseur as well as a buyer." She laughed heartily. "I know your husband better than you." She patted her belly. "He enjoyed it with choucroute. Would you like some for lunch?"

Claire's appetite was nonexistent for pigs' parts and sauerkraut, but she still needed to get information about Sophie. "Perhaps in a little while. Please tell me about the Soltner vintages."

Madame Justine leaned back and crossed her arms before her ample bosom. "Everyone wonders if her brother has Sophie's talents."

"Sophie...is the vintner?"

"Was."

"Why no longer?" A frisson of dread slid through Claire. Had the vineyard been sold? Was the angry man the new owner?

The lines around Madame Justine's eyes deepened. "Your husband does not know?" Tears sat in her eyes.

A chill seized Claire. "What does David not know?"

Justine pushed out her lower lip. "Your husband is good friends with Sophie and her brother. You'd know that if you'd accompanied him once in all the years he came here."

Who was this woman to chastise her? She wanted to toss the remainder of the rare wine at her imperious face, but Claire needed to find Sophie. She swallowed back her words. This woman was right, she knew more about David than Claire did. Nonetheless, she needed to know the truth, and she'd humiliate herself if she had to. "You are correct. But I'm here now, and you'll have to forgive me. Please, tell me what happened?"

Lifting and dropping her shoulders, Justine examined her hands, clasped in prayer. "Sophie died." She blessed herself. "Nearly a year ago."

The words shot through Claire, tearing open the wound David's death had caused. The pain sharpened with the realization that she might never know the truth. "I'm so sorry."

Madame shook her head. "Christmas Eve." She hugged herself. "The grief her son must endure at the happiest time of the year."

"She had a child?" Claire acted surprised. "It must be difficult for her husband also."

Madame cocked her head. "Sophie was the single mother of the boy." She picked up her towel and dried a glass. "And an extraordinary vintner."

At least Justine didn't know David was Luca's father. Claire had to find Luca, without telling Madame Justine any more than she had to. "But what happened to her son?"

"Sophie's brother, Gilbert, adopted him. He treated the boy like a son from the very beginning." She opened a leaded-glass-paned door and placed the glass on a shelf. "But the world awaits the tasting of the next vintage of Château Soltner. We must see if her brother can reproduce Sophie's brilliance."

Was the man she'd angered Gilbert? "Sophie's brother is now the vintner?"

Justine closed her eyes, inhaled, Claire guessed for patience, and nodded.

Claire's shoulders relaxed as she deduced Gilbert was not Sophie's husband. But why had he accused her of wanting to take Luca to America? Did he know David was Luca's father? He must have. Her nerves jangled, making her lips tingle. She might never know how David became Luca's father. She pressed the glass against her lips to calm them and sipped the wine. None of it mattered. The only thing that did matter was her promise to David's spirit: she would deliver his medical records to the child's adopted father—even if he sicced his dog on her—and make him promise to have the boy tested.

A couple entered the dining room, and Justine left the bar to greet them.

Could Claire convince Gilbert to accept David's medical records? She turned the wine glass on the cocktail napkin a quarter turn, and another turn, and another turn. Would the man even listen to her? She'd already lied to him. The truth was her only option. She could only hope he would respect it...and her.

She'd visit again the next morning. Getting Gilbert to listen to her would require more courage than facing his dog.

CHAPTER 10

Jet lag had caught up to her, and having slept till noon, Claire left her hotel after lunch. Not wanting to alert Gilbert of her arrival, she asked the taxi driver to let her out at the foot of the driveway to Château Soltner and to wait for her return. She trudged up the gravel hill. Tall poplars lined either side of the driveway, their icy branches sparkling in the bright sunshine. The afternoon light cast a violet-pink aura over the rolling hills of vineyards, lightly dusted with snow—magical.

She needed some magic. She had rehearsed her speech until she fell asleep the night before. Although her determination was inexhaustible, she had to be careful. Gilbert was angry and obviously threatened if he thought Claire wanted to take Luca to America.

As she reached the courtyard, the bear-of-a-dog barked and leaped to his paws. Claire reached into her pocket, pulled out a bone, and tossed it far beyond him. The beast galloped away and pounced on it.

She clutched her purse, ran to the door, and pulled the metal bell chain. A bright clang shivered in the air.

A scuffling noise came from behind her. Hands on hips, Sophie's brother snorted. "You've returned?"

She brought her hands up. "I lied. I never knew Sophie. My husband did. Actually, he knew her very well, because Sophie sent a photo of Luca to him. And she wrote, 'Our son,' on the back of it."

The anger in his eyes dulled. "Seems you're the last to know."

"The wife always is."

He huffed a laugh. "It is not how you perceive it."

Right. Her hands trembled, and she gripped her purse tightly. "I apologize for lying to you. I thought you were Sophie's husband, and I didn't want to be the one to tell you your son was not yours."

He smoothed his moustache. "Why are you here?"

"David—"

"Get. Out. Now." His voice was low and menacing.

She pulled the large envelope from her purse and extended it. "These are David's medical records. Luca could have inherited David's heart condition. If so, the sooner it is discovered, the easier it is to treat. Please take them."

He crossed his arms and looked down upon her like she was a banana slug.

"Fine." If she gave the envelope to the dog, Gilbert would have to take it away. She clapped her hands and shouted, "Remy, come."

"He doesn't speak English."

The dog bounded to her. She waved the envelope. "Fetch." She flung the envelope like a frisbee, and the dog ran for it.

"Apparently, he can translate. Please take Luca to be tested. If he inherited David's heart condition, he could

die of a heart attack at a very young age, like David did."
Tears stung, but she would not cry. Poor Luca having to
live with such a jerk.

Gilbert ran after the dog and after a bit of tugging,
prized the envelope and opened it.

She didn't even know Gilbert, and she hated him. Yet, he
had adopted her husband's son. There must be some good
in him. She'd failed again. She needed another strategy.
She wasn't leaving France without ensuring that Luca was
tested.

"I'm sorry I don't speak French, but did you hear what
I said?"

He paged through the documents.

"Can you fathom that Luca's life is in danger? Children
that are only five years old can die of this condition. You
need to have Luca tested!" she shouted. She walked toward
him, tripped over a rock, frozen in an ice-covered puddle,
and stumbled. "Merde." At least she knew how to swear in
French. She regained her balance.

"Arrêtez!" His footsteps scuffled. "Wait!"

She glared at the jerk.

"David...died?" He gripped the envelope. His angry eyes
reddened. What she thought might be anguish washed
over his face.

She exhaled, searching for calm. "My husband passed
away, from a heart attack—a little over a year ago. I only
recently discovered the photo of Luca."

His eyes dulled. "I'm deeply sorry."

"Thank you." Tears swelled.

The lines around his eyes softened. "He would have liked to see Luca grow up."

"You knew my husband?" She swallowed against a creeping tightness in her throat.

"Quite well. Sophie got sick, I'd been begging her to see a doctor, and when she did, her doctor gave her three months to live. David usually visited in October, and Sophie wanted to tell him in person. But things spun out of control, and she died, and then I realized I hadn't seen David since before she was diagnosed." His arms fell to his sides. "By the time I tried to contact David his phone number was not in service, and I never received a reply to my emails. When I called the corporate office, I was told he was no longer with the company. And I don't have his personal email or home address."

"David died of a heart condition Luca could have inherited. There are no symptoms. You must have Luca tested." She dizzied and bent over.

He grabbed her hand. "Luca will be arriving soon, and we must talk another time. I don't want him to know of this now. I will help you to your taxi. You could slip." Holding her arm, he walked her down the hill.

Sparks flurried in her vision like snowflakes. She couldn't fight him, couldn't make demands, she could barely walk. Her heart thrashed against her ribs.

He opened the taxi door. "I'm sorry I cannot explain further right now, but I will meet you at your hotel tomorrow morning. L'hôtel la Rivière?"

"Yes, that's my hotel." She allowed him to hold her arm as she got in. "Tomorrow?" Her voice sounded like a plea, and she hated it.

"At nine." He slammed the door and headed back up the hill.

As the driver pulled onto the road, a school bus chugged past them, came to a stop, and opened its doors. Claire opened the window and watched her husband's son run up the hill after his uncle.

CHAPTER 11

After a restless night, Claire drank a pot of coffee to sharpen her mind. Holding onto the banister to calm her jitters, she descended the steps to the hotel reception area. Sophie's brother scrunched his knitted cap as he waited. His bright blue-gray eyes alighting on hers, he dashed toward her.

"Forgive me. I've not properly introduced myself." He extended his hand. "I am Gilbert Soltner."

"Jeel...?" Claire tried to wrap her lips around his name. Madame Justine had said, 'Gilbert.' "We don't have that name in English."

He laughed. "Americans say 'Gilbert.' But in France we say, 'Jeel-bear,' with a soft 'G.'"

"Ah. The French pronunciation is beautiful." She shook his hand. "Jeel-bear."

"Bon. Let us go to a place where we can speak privately. Would you like an Alsatian breakfast? I know of a wonderful patisserie."

She liked this Jeel-bear far more than the man she'd met the day before. "Yes."

He offered his elbow, and she held it as they walked through Petite Venise, the medieval Old Town of Colmar.

Half-timbered buildings with steeply pitched roofs of ter-racotta tiles lined the canals. Windows in every building displayed Christmas: Gnomes, teddy bears, stars, orna-ments, straw animals, giant ginger people. Stuffed white storks with red ribbons around their necks bedecked every souvenir shop.

They entered an alleyway, and Gilbert opened a dark red door with a white lace curtain covering its window. Bells clanged a cheery jingle, and the scent of baking butter and sugar and chocolate enticed her to enter a cave-like dining room filled with pine chairs and tables. Gilbert led them to the back where niches and shelves were carved out of the butter-yellow rock walls.

"What *was* this place?" she asked.

"This cave was part of a farmhouse, where they kept animals." He ran his hand along the ledge of a large in-dentation. "This was where they put hay and grain for the animals to feed. The higher, smaller shelves were for candles and lanterns."

"It's so very old and charming. I'm glad it has been preserved."

He pulled out a chair for her. "May I order an Alsatian specialty for you?"

"Please." She pulled off her scarf and coat.

He called out to a young woman wearing a lacey white blouse and red apron. He spoke in French, and she hurried to the kitchen.

She returned and placed a bottle of clear liquid and two short glasses on the table.

Gilbert poured. "This is a local clear brandy, not the stuff tourists buy in the market. This Mirabelle is very special."

Claire never had brandy so early in the day, but she sipped. "Umm. Sweet yet fresh and a bit of a tart taste. Are Mirabelle plums yellow?"

"Yes." Gilbert's eyebrows rose. "Did David help you to train your palate?"

A memory of David feeding her a Mirabelle plum while her eyes were closed made her smile. "I suppose he did." She took another sip. "This is a bit strong for me so early in the day. May I have a cappuccino?"

"A café crème. Certainly."

The waitress delivered the coffee and two plates of plum tarte.

"I left a message at the hotel yesterday. I felt badly about the way I *welcomed* you."

"I was out all day yesterday and didn't get your call. I was shopping for fabrics and got back pretty late." She placed a napkin on her lap. "The last time I was in France, nearly thirty years ago, I bought so much I had to ship cartons of fabrics to my friend Marti. I might still have some left."

He laughed. "Did you go to Tissus aux Deux RR?"

She shook her head. "Tell me more."

"They have the best home décor fabrics." He rubbed his palms along his thighs. "After Sophie passed, I needed something to take my mind from her and wine, something Luca and I could to together. So, we began redecorating the château and had great fun choosing colors. We finished the grand salon and the first of twelve guest bedrooms.

We have much more to do. But now that Luca is back at school, I think he is relieved he no longer has time for this project."

"Do you make the drapes and cover the furniture, yourself?"

"Oh, no. I work with a retired woman who was a tailor. She enjoys sewing and earning a bit of money, and I enjoy her company. She has great experience and excellent skills. Do you sew other things besides maillots?"

"How do you know—"

"David bragged quite a bit about your designs."

She smiled a sad smile and nodded. "I design drapes, pillow shams, tablecloths, clothing. I enjoy the challenges of working with different fabrics."

"Ah, yes, velvet has a..." he ran his fingers back and forth along the table, "you call it a nap?"

"Yes, and because of the nap it changes color."

"Ask me how I know of this quality."

She laughed in sympathy. "So, sorry. That's one mistake you make only once."

"Fortunately, the store still had a few meters left and now the chair arms are all the same color. And I am grateful to the salesperson who explained you need more fabric for the matching of plaid before I purchased thirty meters."

"Excellent advice. I'll have to visit that store."

He raised his glass. "I am happy to take you."

A current of warmth tingled with excitement moved through Claire. She'd never discussed fabrics or design with David. She and Gilbert shared an enthusiasm and interest for both.

Gilbert's smile waned. "If my wines are not as good as Sophie's, I will sell the grapes to other wineries. I will have to turn the château and vineyard into an event space and wedding venue, and all the rooms will need to be redecorated."

"Are you worried your wines won't sell?

He shrugged. "I think I make a fine wine, but Sophie's were—" he kissed his fingertips, "exquisite!"

"In America we say, 'She's a hard act to follow.'" Claire dug into the ruby-red fruit tarte. "Mmm…This is exquisite!" She was stalling. "I'm afraid I am at a disadvantage here. I hoped to meet Sophie so she could explain how David is Luca's father. Perhaps I'm being a bit stupid, but I'd like to know the truth if you know it—if you don't mind." Her voice squeaked. She took another huge bite of the tarte, as if it might give her courage to hear the truth.

"I apologize for my rudeness the other day. I suspected you were David's wife the moment I saw you. He spoke often of you, about how beautiful and intelligent and funny you are and how proud he was of your determination to invent a…life-saving swimsuit?"

She smiled through sadness.

"After not hearing from him after Sophie's diagnosis, and we'd not seen or heard from him in more than a year, I feared he had learned of Sophie's death and sent you to investigate so he could take Luca away. After all, he was Luca's birth father, but I panicked and behaved badly. I apologize."

"I get your point."

"I have legally adopted Luca in France, which I hope is respected in the United States."

"I would never take anyone's child." Her words rushed. Although she didn't know the truth about how Luca came to be, she did know her husband was honorable. "And if David made a promise, he would never go back on his word."

"I know what you say about David is true. He was a very good friend to me and Sophie. We would not have enjoyed the success we've had without him. He had a good and kind heart. I'm terribly sorry he has passed." He inhaled deeply, his eyes reddening. "The news was a shock to me, and I am deeply sorry for my own loss of a very dear friend. And the loss to Luca and you."

"Thank you." She swallowed against tears. "Can you please explain from the beginning? Were—" she swallowed a hard lump. "Were David and Sophie...?"

He downed his brandy. "David bought our wines for a popular boutique wine store outside of New York City. They kept ordering more of our wines, and David continued to taste and order new ones for them, twice a year. He was very curious about my winemaking methods, and I enjoyed demonstrating them. We had, what you call, a camaraderie?"

She nodded.

"One day I was cooking a cassoulet, and he'd said it was his favorite French dish, so I invited him to stay. Sophie joined us for dinner and, perhaps because we all had much to drink, Sophie complained that all the men she dated were not to her liking, and she just wanted to have a child.

She had investigated using a donor, but she lamented that the most important quality she wanted in the father of her child was to have a good heart and that quality could not be determined in a profile."

The realization that Sophie's desire for a child was opposite of Claire's spurred a squirming in Claire's stomach. David found a woman who wanted the same thing he did. "She deeply desired a child."

Gilbert nodded, poured himself more brandy, and offered Claire another pour.

She shook her head, thinking there was no man as good hearted as her David, even if it was his damaged heart that killed him.

Gilbert stared at the brandy. "I said, 'You mean a good heart, like David's?' I was joking, but Sophie's look was serious." He crossed his arms. "David's face grew serious also, and when Sophie saw it, she made a joke and said she'd continue to interview men. Maybe she would run an advertisement. She did not want the man in the child's life. Surely some man would find that package attractive."

"One would think." Claire held very still, fortifying herself for the blade of truth.

Gilbert broke off a piece of tarte. "The next morning, David visited us in the cave. He told Sophie that he would agree to be a donor if she wanted. She should think it through and if agreeable, let him know when he returned. But Sophie didn't need any thinking-time, she immediately agreed. She also promised she'd hire an attorney to draw up an agreement and make an appointment for David at the fertility clinic to make a donation—only for her—during his next business trip."

Claire's heart squeezed as she closed her eyes, memories of David's kind eyes and dimpled smile warming her. Why hadn't David told her? He'd not had a physical affair—but wasn't *not* telling her about his son almost as much of a betrayal? She didn't want to be angry with him, but heat pulsed up her back.

Gilbert pulled a large envelope from his jacket pocket. "Both David and Sophie wrote letters to Luca for him to read on his eighteenth birthday. I made copies for you."

She stopped chewing, the tangy fruit stinging her tongue. The thought of touching the envelope made her hands grow cold.

He pushed the envelope across the table. "A copy of their agreement is also in there."

She looked at it as if it were a sleeping snake.

He sipped his brandy. "You should know that, initially, Sophie didn't want Luca to know David was his father. That was a specific clause in the contract."

The pulsing heat washed through her. "But David wanted children more than anything."

"I was not privy to their discussion, but I think that because this is a very small town, and Sophie is well known, she didn't want everyone to think that she and David were lovers. Eventually, Luca began asking about his father. Sophie asked David, and they decided to tell him, despite their original agreement."

Claire pulled back. She searched for the power to speak, but her words jumbled, sticking in her mouth. "David...met...Luca?"

He nodded. "Luca was only a few months old the first time David met him. He visited many times, during which Luca didn't know that David was his father. But when Luca learned David was his father, he was overjoyed." Gilbert downed the rest of his brandy. "He calls him 'Papa David.'" Pride sat in Gilbert's eyes.

A whooshing sound filled Claire's head. The room closed around her. David had known and loved his child for seven years and never told her. How could he leave his son? Why did he keep her out of their relationship?

Gilbert cleared his throat. "Luca lost his mother nearly a year ago, on Christmas Eve. I cannot tell him he's also lost his father. That is why I wanted you to leave yesterday. I wanted to discuss this with you, without Luca present."

Sparks of light swirled. Why hadn't David told her? He'd kept the birth of his son, the boy calling him Papa David, this enchanting little seven-year-old boy—someone he loved at least as much if not more than he loved her—a secret from her for nearly eight years? She hunched over as her lungs caved around her aching heart.

She grabbed her coat and pulled it over her shoulders. Gripping the chairback, she struggled to stand. "I'm sorry. I...can't...I need...I can't be here right now."

She grabbed her purse and fled out the door, down the alley, across a square, sliding on the icy cobblestones, searching for her hotel. She crossed a wooden bridge but couldn't remember if they'd crossed it coming to the patisserie. She ran along the quay, sliding in the snow. How could she not remember the address of the hotel where she spent her honeymoon? It was near the river.

She hid behind a brightly lighted Christmas tree and pulled out her phone. She had saved the hotel address and requested directions, but she couldn't decide whether the app was telling her to go right or left.

The way to the left was across a bridge. Nope, she wasn't going anywhere near water.

She ran a block to the right and was wrong. She retraced her steps and stood at the foot of the bridge. Roiling water rushed along, shelves of ice clinging to the quay. She inhaled, squeezed her eyes shut, and bolted across the wooden bridge. As her feet hit cobblestones, she opened her eyes to the hotel shimmering in the distance. She spun around, making sure Gilbert was not near, and ran all the way to her room. Why did David keep his son a secret?

CHAPTER 12

Slamming the door behind her, Claire ripped off her coat and stabbed her phone's speed dial for Marti, praying she was still awake.

"Claire! How are—"

"David met his son, at least a dozen times!" Claire moaned and fell onto the bed, trembling. "Why didn't he tell me?"

"Take a deep breath and push out the air slowly."

Claire inhaled but erupted in sobs.

"Try again. Do it with me." Marti counted as she slowly exhaled.

The shaking subsided as Claire slowed her breathing.

"Start from the beginning."

Claire dragged the sheet across her wet face and stared up at the wooden beams crossing the ceiling. "Sophie wanted a sperm donor, but she had trouble finding a man with a good heart. No one was more good-hearted than David." She swallowed against tears. "So, David volunteered, but they had an agreement, a contract that specified that Sophie would take full responsibility for the child and neither of them were to let the child know that David was the father until the child turned eighteen."

"They drew up an agreement?"

"Yes, her brother gave me a copy." She bolted up, searching for the envelope. "Damn, I forgot the envelope Jeel-Bear gave me."

"Jeel-Bear? When did you start speaking French?"

"We say, Gilbert, but he taught me how to say it in French."

"It's so beautiful in French. And romantic."

"Right, so they signed an agreement, David made the donation at a fertility clinic, and she gave birth to Luca." A sob escaped. "We were right—he didn't cheat." She sucked in air and slowly pushed out her exhalation. "He met Luca when he was a few months old, and he visited him on every one of his business trips. Finally, Luca began asking who his father was, and they told him. He calls him Papa David." A cry escaped, a cry of sorrow and appreciation of the child's affection for her husband.

"So, learning that he had a son was not a shock that contributed to David's heart attack?"

"It was Sitosterolemia that killed David." A torrent of tears hit Claire. "That poor little boy has lost both his parents. Sophie died last Christmas Eve."

"Oh, no. That poor child."

Claire bolted up. "But why didn't David tell me he had a son?" Tears dripped from her chin, and she swiped at them. "This is going to sound crazy from a woman who postponed having kids most of her life, but I feel left out." She dropped back onto the bed and sobbed.

"David wanted kids more than anything. How could he have only seen Luca twice a year? He must have adored

Luca. And how could he have kept this wonderful secret he held so dearly from me?" She punched the bed. "David kept half his life from me. And I feel selfish and guilty because it's all my own fault."

"David was always protective of you, Claire. He probably didn't tell you because he didn't want to hurt you."

"But keeping a secret from me hurts! And Luca missing his father must have hurt him, too." She hated how her voice was whining. "Isn't that a betrayal? Because let me tell you, I feel betrayed!" The tone of her voice dropped so low it sounded like she was growling.

"How do you think you might have felt if he had told you?"

"Guilty." The word exploded, surprising Claire. "I'd have felt guilty for not giving him the children he so very much wanted." She rolled over. "I might have worried he would leave me for Luca's mother."

Mariah Carey's *All I want for Christmas is You* playing in the courtyard made her want to rip out the speakers. She got up and pulled the drapes closed.

"Don't you think David would have wanted to protect you from feeling guilty or insecure?"

The pout on her lips made her feel like a child. "Yes."

"Hmmm..." Marti made soft cooing sounds.

A writhing in Claire's gut built pressure that reached her eyes. Collapsing onto the soft down-filled comforter, she let the tears flow as she stared at the same ceiling that they'd lain under on their honeymoon night. The irony. "I feel like my marriage was based on lies."

"Oh, Claire, your marriage was based in the profound love you had for one another. No marriage is perfect. It seems you both lied to protect the other."

That truth squeezed her heart. David's lie and betrayal were all her fault because she'd lied to him. She'd told him she wasn't ready to have kids when the truth was she feared becoming a mother.

"Claire?"

"Huh?"

"Are you okay?"

"Yeah. I'm so confused and tired. I wish I had some of that brandy Jeel-Bear had ordered at the patisserie."

Marti laughed. "It's going to take you a long time to process all of this. I wish I were there to help you. Are you going to meet Luca?"

"I don't know. When I learned that David knew and spent time with Luca, I freaked out and ran from the restaurant."

"Take some time and then call Jeel-Bear. He seems like he would like to help you."

"Ugh." Claire pushed herself up.

"Wouldn't you like to meet David's son?"

"Luca must be missing David terribly. But I think I might have a meltdown." She smoothed the quilt. "I never knew my father, so I never missed him. Except when fathers arrived at the convent to pick up their daughters, the girls running into their arms, squealing with delight, their fathers beaming with pride. I'd never had that experience, and, as it was so foreign to me, I found it more interesting than a sense of longing."

"Take it one step at a time. Just allow yourself to feel all that you feel, and then you can sort it out."

"Thank you, Marti. I don't know what I'd do without you."

"I'm always here for you. I love you. And I can't wait to celebrate Christmas together."

Claire groaned. "I haven't even booked a ticket home. I'll have to fly standby again. One crisis at a time. I don't know if or when Gilbert will let me meet Luca. And if he will, I don't know if I really want to meet him, although I'm pretty sure I do...of course I want to meet him, I just hope I have the courage." She wiped her face. "At least I gave Gilbert David's medical records so Luca can be tested."

"Take a nap and then go enjoy the Christmas markets. David would want you to. And call me if you need to talk."

"Thanks. I will." Claire turned off her phone. Images of David playing with his son swirled in her mind and bruised her heart. She wouldn't be able to sleep. She washed her face, put on her coat, and headed for the markets. Maybe she could find a toy for Luca for Christmas.

CHAPTER 13

Walking out into the brisk air and bright sunshine cleared Claire's vision. She tried to ignore her own voice, taunting her: It was her fault David had kept Luca a secret—she was the one who procrastinated having children until it was too late. A tiny fissure opened in her heart and love for David blossomed through the old pain. She was glad David had had a son in his life, even if it wasn't her who gave birth to him.

Clouds scuttled, dimming the sunshine. Was she really glad? She wished with all her heart he'd been able to spend more time with Luca. And that he had shared Luca with her.

Blue and white lights crisscrossed towering evergreens that lined the ancient buildings, welcoming her to the Christmas market. Along the cobbled streets wooden huts with red and white striped awnings displayed glass ornaments, wooden toys, wreaths of rosemary and lavender, woolen hats and mittens. She skirted the scent of sauerkraut and grilled sausages, following her nose to copper pots of steaming Vin Rouge Chaud, a warm, spiced red wine served in mugs.

Crowds jostled her as she purchased a cup of wine and sipped. David would say the wine was a bit raw, but the spices were complex and interesting. The memory of their first cup together brought her to a stop. He'd been educating her palate since the beginning. She sipped again and found the cloves bitter and the cinnamon overcooked and a bit woody.

The sky darkened and a chill breeze fluttered the red and white awnings. As she walked between the stalls, a gray-haired woman smiled from a booth, offering a sample of cheese. Claire accepted it and chewed. Munster, the regional specialty. Strong, but it complemented the wine. "Merci."

David loved traveling to France, but after his son was born, he must have loved it all the more. Knowing how David loved kids, she could not fathom how he managed to leave Luca.

The joyous sounds of the crowd irritated her. Why did they have to shout?

Glass ornaments shivered in the cold, tinkling like bells. After he'd made his final invitation to join him in France, when she proclaimed she wasn't ready to have children, David must have felt Sophie's offer was his last chance to have a child. The reflection of her face in a scarlet round ornament stretched her cheeks like a clown's. She rubbed her eyes. She'd been such a fool.

The licorice scent of anise in the wine grew cloying. She threw the rest of the wine in a trash can.

The aroma of sauerkraut pricked her nose. People closed in around her, waiting for their plates of choucroute. She pushed her way around them. Had she used her life-saving swimsuit obsession as an excuse not to have children?

A little girl twirled her cone of peppermint candy floss high in the air, whacking Claire's coat sleeve, which was now covered in a streak of sticky pink sugar. The child screamed with glee. The cacophony of languages clashed against booming American Christmas songs. It was good to know that Crosby and Sinatra were still popular in France, but didn't Édith Piaf record any Noël albums?

Stalls selling hand-carved wooden toys reminded her of Luca. Seven was too old for wooden trains and soldiers, wasn't it? Sadness tinted her imaginings of David playing with his son and caused her to stumble. She would have enjoyed being with them. Or would she? How would she have felt? Left out? Jealous? Regretful? Would she have begun to long for her unknown father? She turned around, searching for an exit, but a display caught her eye.

A long wooden stall filled with marionettes that looked like reindeer, elves, cats, dogs, and birds lured her. A balding, white-whiskered man, wearing a leather apron embossed with white flowers and red berries, reached up and removed a cross of pine sticks with myriad strings attached. He climbed up on a stool and began working the sticks and strings. A black and brown furry dog sprang to life, cocking his head toward Claire and wagging his tail.

He looked just like Remy and was nearly as big. Uh-oh. Too late to back up. The puppet dog galumphed along the counter, his fur shivering, his tongue lolling, his large round eyes staring right at her. Before Claire could pull away, the dog's paws pounced on her arm, his velvet-soft tongue licked her face, and he leaned his head upon her shoulder, his long eyelashes batting around his big brown eyes in total flirtation.

She laughed. "Adorable."

The puppeteer peered down. "He likes you." He jiggled the sticks, making the dog's tail wag in delight.

She ran her hand over the dog's soft fur. "I like him, too."

"Very reasonably priced."

"He would be a unique Christmas gift." Claire continued to pet the puppet as if he were Remy.

"For a little boy or girl? Or a big boy?"

Claire blinked at the vendor, wondering at his insightfulness. "Big and little boy." Visions of Gilbert and Luca playing with the puppet dog and teasing Remy made her smile. She would also get some treats for Remy. "Can you wrap him, please?"

"First I must show you how to work him, so you can all play together." He climbed off his stool and held out the sticks.

Why had she not included herself in her imaginings? Did she not want to meet David's son? She'd only seen a photo of Luca and her heart squeezed with longing to meet him. Longing faded to regret, and she blamed herself for missing out on an opportunity she prevented with her own fear.

The man wrapped a string around her pinky, showing her how to wag the dog's tail. He taught her how to tilt and rotate the sticks to make the dog walk and pounce and sit. What if Gilbert didn't want her to meet Luca? What if Luca didn't like her? Her heartbeat quickened. She was feeling desperate. She wanted more than anything to meet David's child. She wanted to know David through his son, the part of her husband she'd missed.

She swallowed against a tightening in her throat. "He's so handsome. What is his name?"

"Oh, Madame, I carved him, and my wife sewed his fur. If we named him, we would never give him up. It is for your little boy to name him."

Her little boy. Love flowed through Claire, warming her to her toes. She could have felt love like this a long time ago—if she'd not been so fearful.

The man chuckled like Santa himself as he charged her card and tied a ribbon around the box. "Joyeux Noël, Madame."

"Joyeux Noël, Monsieur." She picked up her card and the box. "Did I say that correctly?"

"Bien sûr. Happy Christmas." He rubbed his aproned belly and ho-ho-hoed.

Her water-resistant running shoes slid on the cobbles. The temperature had dropped, and snow was falling. She felt like she was inside a magical toy store. Every window box featured a unique Christmas tableau: reindeer with silver bells hanging from their antlers, Raggedy Ann dolls with red-and-green plaid ribbons on their braids, carved storks wearing red scarves around their necks, puffy gingerbread people and gnomes baking cookies. All adorable, but where did people store all the stuff—or did they keep it up year-round?

Snowflakes drifted lazily, muffling clanging church bells. She'd been happy for the few moments she'd been with the Santa-like vendor, but the heaviness of guilt and betrayal weighed on her. She needed to sit down.

Following the sound of the bells, she came upon a narrow curving street which she followed to a square. Medieval buildings towered around her. A pyramid of Christmas trees twinkling with white lights filled the fountain. A clutch of nativity statues stood in a nook, a soft drift of snow filling the empty cradle awaiting the Christ child.

The tall wooden doors of a church loomed beyond the fountain. She blew into her hands, warming them. She hadn't been honest with David, but it was time to be honest with herself.

Chapter 14

Although it was a small church in the old part of town, its carved wooden door was as grand as the cathedral's. Claire slipped into the still darkness where flickering candles reminded her of fireflies in the meadows of Vermont.

Incense burned the same aroma as it did in America, reminiscent of burning fall leaves. Rows of red and green glass votive candleholders glowed at the feet of a statue of the Virgin. Claire dropped a coin in a metal box and lit a candle in a green glass—David's favorite color. She knelt, made the sign of the cross. The flames flickered. She whispered, "I pray Luca did not inherit your condition."

Just to her right stood a confessional with dark red curtains covering the cubicle door openings.

Claire sat on a nearby wooden chair, remembering she felt just as cold in the Vermont church. A brass bookstand and candleholders glittered on the altar, and, in an ornate vase, a bouquet of flowers seemed to be shivering. White lights blinked on the two Christmas trees behind a nativity scene of life-sized statues.

She hugged herself and sighed a puff of steam. She'd come in here to be honest with herself, certainly not to get warm. Despite the kind nuns and all the friends she'd made, she was always lonely during the holidays—until she met David. Now she'd lost him, her job, and possibly her home if David's estate wasn't settled when she returned. Who was going to hire a fifty-year-old woman who was obsessed with a life-preserver swimsuit design? The pain she'd stowed in her heart leaked out, leaving sticky guilt in its tracks. She longed to understand why David hadn't told her about his son. In the deepest part of her heart, she knew he hid Luca to protect her, but that fact didn't dull her sense of betrayal.

The pain mounted, and she knew she was to blame. Why had she not given him children? Having kids was his dream. But as the years passed, he spoke less and less about them. Until he ceased mentioning becoming a dad. Was that because he had become one, and she didn't know about it?

An elderly priest poked his head out of the confessional and looked about. He spotted her, smiled, and hooked his finger at her, indicating he was ready to hear her confession. He pulled his head back behind the drape.

The lump in her throat grew larger. Being honest with herself required courage she didn't have, but she needed to know her own truth. She grabbed the chairback and, checking to ensure no one else was waiting for the priest, she picked up her box and strode to the confessional, pulled open the curtain, and slipped into the empty cubicle.

She knelt before the dark screen, behind which sat a tall male figure. She blessed herself and erupted. "Bless me Father for I have sinned, it has been so many years since my last confession, I have no idea when it was, but these are my sins, I lied—"

"You do not speak French?" The man's voice was gentle yet gravelly with age.

"I'm afraid not."

"You are from America?"

"Is that another sin?"

He chuckled. "No. If you speak slowly, I will be able to follow you."

"Okay." She made the sign of the cross. "Bless me Father for—"

"You do not have to do all that again. You said you told a lie?"

"A big one."

"To whom?"

The priests in America followed the Bless-me-Father formula; none asked for specifics. "I lied to my husband."

"About?"

Claire gripped the edges of her coat sleeves. The truth poked at her like a sharp icicle. "I told him I wanted children. He really wanted them, and I told him I did too."

"And you don't?"

"I put my career first and was always traveling and too busy and then it was too late."

"So, you lied to yourself, also?"

Her heartbeat thrummed in her ears. Her protestations of: *the time to have a child was never ideal* rang in her head. All that time—she lied—not only to David but also to herself. "I guess so, although I don't think I was aware of it at the time. I'm not proud of it, but I guess I didn't really want children, otherwise I would have made sure it happened."

"And you were afraid to tell your husband the truth?"

"Mmm-hmm." Her mouth dried.

"What did you fear?"

Sounds like crashing waves pounded in her ears. Why didn't he just prescribe five *Hail Marys* and be done with it? "I—I was afraid if I told him…, he wouldn't love me anymore." She pressed her fingers against her lips, holding back a sob. Where had that come from? Was it true?

"Mmm. Do you really think he would have stopped loving you?"

"No." Her rapid reply surprised her. But that didn't mean she wasn't afraid of the possibility, however unlikely. She couldn't live without David's love. Even now, the memory of his love kept her buoyed like a life jacket.

"Can you tell him the truth now?'

"No," she cried. "He passed away." Her sob escaped. "And he never knew."

The priest made comforting humming sounds. "What do you think he might say if you could tell him now?'

"He'd be so disappointed in me." She wiped her eyes.

"Why don't you try imagining him? Remember how much he loved you and see if you can tell him."

She stared at the screen, hoping the man behind it saw only her silhouette, like she could only see his. She imagined David's soft brown eyes, filled with love and caring. She had thought he'd be angry, but he opened his arms and stretched them toward her. "David?" she whispered. "I thought…I thought I wanted children, but I didn't, and

I didn't know it then, but I know now that I didn't, but it wasn't because of the children, I was afraid, I think, because I didn't want to be like my mother." She gulped a breath. "I didn't know it then, and I'm so, so sorry." She closed her eyes, feeling him embrace her, enclosing her with his strong arms, his lips pressed to her forehead. He released her, and his warmth left her like a retreating tide.

Her arms ached with longing. "I think he forgives me. I'm not sure."

"I think he does, and I hope in time you will forgive yourself."

"For lying, you mean?"

"Lying to someone when you know the truth is a lie. But if you are also lying to yourself as well as the other person, it's not as big a lie. Do you know why you lied to yourself?"

"No. I must have been so convincing, even I believed myself."

"It takes great courage to explore why one lies to herself. But now that you have admitted that you did lie, perhaps learning why won't be too difficult."

"I hope not." She pulled a tissue from her pocket and wiped her face. "Thank you, Father. You're probably going to have me pray a rosary for my penance." She huffed a laugh.

"I think there is something that might help you more than a rosary."

Not wanting her to do her penance? What kind of priest was this man? "In America, there is always penance. Is that not so in France?"

"Yes, but in this case, there is something I think would be more helpful to you. One of our nuns is from Canada. She misses speaking English. Sister Georgette would love to share a cup of tea and a conversation with an English-speaker. She also bakes cookies that are so delicious they are sold in the market. I'm sure she'd share some and enjoy a visit with you."

The last thing Claire wanted to do was talk with a nun who would remind her of all the years she spent at boarding school. "Of course, Father. I'd be happy to." A stickiness rose in her throat. She hadn't even finished her confession and was lying again already.

"When you leave by the great doors, turn to your left and ring the bellpull at the right of the blue door."

"I'm sure I can find it." She would turn right, pretend to be confused, and flee. Yet another lie, and she wasn't even out of the confessional. She'd pray two *Act of Contritions*.

"I absolve you of your sins. I'll give you a blessing in French if you don't mind."

"Merci, Father." She bowed her head.

His blessing sounded like a soft carol. When he finished, he wished her a happy Christmas.

"Joyeux Noël, Father." Her wish sounded like an apology for not visiting Sister Georgette.

Claire hurried down the side aisle but stopped before David's candle. She knelt and watched the flame waver. Returning to his image in her mind, she asked him: Do you know why I lied to myself? His smile glowed with compassion and empathy and love.

Figuring out that part was going to hurt—she knew it.

She rose, blessed herself and headed to the door, just as a tall priest, buttoning his cape, arrived beside it. He smiled. "Are you looking for Sister Georgette?"

She recognized the priest's voice. Was this man a mind reader? Did he know she planned to do the opposite of what he'd asked? She was a terrible person, lying to a priest. She swallowed her guilt and nodded.

"I'll show you the way." He touched her elbow and gently guided her out into the snow.

CHAPTER 15

A petite woman with eyes bright as a robin's peered around the massive wooden door. "Père Mathéo!"

"Sister, I'd like you to meet an American who would love to have a chat in English in exchange for some of your delicious cookies."

The woman brought her fingers to her mouth to hide her smile and blushed like a teen despite her graying hair. "Will you join us, Père?"

"No, I am expected at the stall to sell those cookies for a few hours. Enjoy yourselves."

Claire's heart buoyed with her realization that she would not be chatting with two people of the cloth.

As the door closed, the woman's gnarly hand grasped Claire's. "Welcome. I'm Sister Georgette, and I'm nearly done with the batter. Won't you join me for a cup of tea?"

"Thank you. I'm Claire." She pressed the balls of her feet into the cold stone floor, wishing she could flee. She was barely holding onto her emotions, couldn't identify all of them, and feared that if this nun was as gentle and kind as the nuns at the convent, she'd no longer be able to dam up her feelings.

Sister Georgette led her to a rickety chair before a long, scarred wooden table laden with bowls of flour, eggs, butter, brown sugar, nuts, dried cherries, apricots, and raisins. A dark brown bottle of alcohol sat in the center of it all.

"Do you like fruitcake?"

Claire's teeth ached at the thought. She rested her hand on the back of the chair and readied to make a run for the door. "Uh..."

Sister's laughter tinkled like glass wind chimes. "Yes, I mean those dense bricks of sickeningly sweet glacé fruit studded with rubbery nuts."

Claire laughed. "No, I don't."

Sister whispered, "Neither do I."

Claire smiled and sat opposite the bowls of dried fruit.

Sister placed a cup of tea before her. "Sugar?"

"No, merci."

"Where in America do you live?"

"Seattle."

Sister Georgette washed her hands, dried them, and returned to a huge bowl sitting on the end of the table. "Ah, the Pacific Northwest. I lived in Quebec, very mountainous, like Seattle." She dragged a wooden spoon, nearly the size of an oar, through the stiff batter. "What brings you to France?"

Claire wished for a cup of the brandy. So many feelings were cartwheeling through her, she feared they'd erupt. The nuns at her boarding school always wiggled out what was troubling her, and that was exactly what this one was doing with her kind voice. Claire didn't want to have an emotional breakdown with this poor woman. "The Christmas markets."

"Just magical, aren't they?"

The memory of the puppet man's jovial demonstration of the dog brought a smile. "Very magical."

"Did you make Christmas cookies with your mother?"

Claire squirmed in the straight-backed chair. She did not want to discuss her mother, nor did she want to volunteer she had attended boarding school in the state bordering Quebec province. "No, but I did bake them with friends."

"What kind?"

A laugh escaped her at the memory of her inexperience leading to both burned and undercooked treats. "Snowballs?"

"Ah, Pfeffernüsse!"

"Well, these were Italian, and I didn't really make them...I just rolled them in the powdered sugar."

"They were delicious, no?"

"Oh, they melted in my mouth." Another laugh bubbled up. "My friends told all their relatives that I made the cookies as a gift for them." Her mouth dried. "It was the first time I spent Christmas with a family."

Sister Georgette wiped her hands on her apron, left her paddle, and sat next to Claire. "How old were you?"

"Seventeen." She clapped her hand over her mouth. It had been thirty-three years since that day. Strange she shared that memory and allowed this woman so close. But Sister Georgette reminded her of the nuns who'd loved and cared for her.

"What happened to your mother?"

"Oh, I had a mother, but…" She sipped her tea. "She enrolled me in a boarding school when I was about seven. She visited once a year, on Christmas. We had tea in Mother Superior's office, and the nun did most of the talking. My mother answered all her questions with an economy of words. When Mother Superior pointed out how I embroidered the collar of my dress, or pleated my skirt, or hand-painted the buttons, my mother responded with a stiff smile and, 'nice' or 'lovely.'" Claire ran her finger over the pink roses of the teacup. "I imagine the Christmas teas were as stressful to Mother Superior as they were for my mother."

"I am so sorry. Your mother lost the opportunity of loving her beautiful daughter."

The scent of butter and sugar caramelizing eased the ache in Claire, and a melting feeling coated her heart.

"What of your father?"

"I never met him."

"But you had friends?"

"I had many friends at school. I loved sewing, and I taught the other girls how to make outfits for their dolls, and then we all sewed clothes for ourselves." Her laugh surprised her. "We had fashion shows for the nuns. I guess our friendships were bonded in our sewing group. But I was the only one to go to college for design."

"I would have liked to see your fashion shows." Sister sipped her tea. "What happened to your mother?"

"She died when I was seventeen." Claire stared at the brandy.

"I'm so sorry. What happened?"

Claire had no idea how her mother had died. Had she been too shocked to inquire? Had she not cared? "I don't know the details, but my mother appointed a fellow attorney, Lucille, as executor of her estate. Lucille traveled all the way to my boarding school to tell me my mother died. She drove me back to Connecticut and helped me into my mother's house."

Claire wrapped her arms around herself. "The house was empty of life. Empty of memories because we'd never made any. And it was so cold. I asked Lucille if I could go back to the convent to be with the nuns for Christmas, as I always spent the holiday with them. Lucille seemed shocked. She wouldn't hear of my *not* spending Christmas with her and her husband and their families, so I packed a bag, and spent not only Christmas Eve with her and Carmine, but also Christmas Day, Christmas week, the New Year, and Epiphany." The memory warmed her, but a tear dripped, and she swatted at it.

The memory was also like a train, racing ahead and, surprising herself, she got on board for the ride.

"They were so very kind. Carmine made dinner the night I arrived, and it was the best spaghetti and meatballs I'd ever tasted. And then he asked me to help with the cookies." She looked up at Sister's beatific smile. The convent kitchen changed into the Marconi family kitchen as she recalled that Christmas. Lucille and Carmine's arms were wrapped around her. "When we arrived at Lucille's in-laws' home, Carmine announced, 'This is our dear friend, Claire, and she made these herself for you all.'

Aunts, uncles, cousins, grandparents all cheered, every one of them hugging me and kissing my cheek." She basked in the memory of that kitchen, the people, the love. Claire looked up at Sister, wondering why she had trusted her with this memory. "I think I know why you bake cookies. It's a gift of love, isn't it?"

Sister nodded. "Your friends gave you a great gift."

"Many gifts. My first Christmas with a family. They welcomed me, embraced me, appreciated me. I still feel their warmth."

"Will you spend this Christmas with them?"

Claire puffed a sigh. "Lucille and Carmine sent Christmas cards inviting me and my husband to join them every year, but eventually I lost touch with them." Why had she lost that relationship? In a way, they were her first family, something she should have nourished. She'd also lost touch with all the girls she'd sewed with at the convent. She would send Lucille and Carmine a postcard. Snowflakes mounded on fir branches outside the window, just as they had in Vermont. "David and I married, nearby here, in Riq—sorry, I don't know how to pronounce the name of the town."

"Riquewihr. In the tiny chapel?" Her eyes sparkled.

Claire nodded. "On Christmas Eve."

"Where is your husband?"

An ache pierced Claire. "He passed...six-, no, seventeen months ago."

Sister's hands gentled Claire's.

The ache in Claire's heart cracked open. Tears tumbled, and she let them roll down her cheeks.

"You've suffered so many losses." Sister offered a paper napkin.

Claire accepted the napkin and blew her nose. "Father Matéo sent me to speak English with you, and here I am crying."

"We're speaking English, aren't we?" She reached for the bottle. "Would you like a brandy?" She poured it into Claire's teacup.

"You drink while you bake?"

"Oh, heavens, no. I soak the dried fruit in it and pour the remainder into the batter." She poured a splash for herself and held up her teacup. "Brandy is the only good thing in fruitcake, so I borrowed that ingredient for the cookies." She giggled like a teenager and clinked her teacup against Claire's.

"May I try one?"

"Certainly." Sister retrieved a brown box tied with red-and-white twine and placed it before her. "For you."

"Merci." Claire opened the box, and the aroma of cinnamon swaddled her. She plucked up a lumpy golden-brown cookie and took a tiny bite. Nutmeg and cinnamon teased her tastebuds, and the crumbly dough melted on her tongue. "It's light as an angel. The dates are the silkiness?"

Sister nodded.

Claire took another bite. Chewed a soft raisin, hinting brandy. "The slight tang of apricot, tart fresh cranberry, rich dark cherry, a nuttiness." She rolled her tongue, chasing a hint of spice—cloves. She swallowed. "This is the most delicious cookie I've ever tasted."

Sister Georgette's face glowed. "I've been working on the recipe for more than thirty-five years. I'm so glad you like them."

"But cranberries are North American. And they are such a surprise. Just when you think you've tasted something tart, the taste flees, and you must take another bite to find the tartness again."

Her tinkling laugh was like a silver bell. "We had them in Quebec. I must order them here."

Claire reached for another cookie. "How do you make them so light with all the fruit and nuts in them?"

"The egg whites and baking soda are doing their jobs." She looked deeply into Claire's eyes. "You have a remarkably sensitive palate."

"My husband trained me. He studied as a sommelier. If you can taste things in wine, you can taste them in food, even in the air." Claire took another cookie and offered one.

"Oh, no. I've become inured. I've been baking since the beginning of November, and I think I've begun to smell like them. I'll get a craving for them around Easter."

They laughed together.

"That's not such a bad thing," Claire said. "May I buy a box?"

Sister put her hands up. "That is my gift to you."

"I mean I'd like to buy another box...for the owners of my hotel. They've been keeping an eye out for me, and I'd like to bring them a gift." She thought that was a plausible excuse. She couldn't tell Sister she hoped to give the cookies to the uncle of her husband's son.

"I'll take you to the stall where the Sisters sell them. It's right outside the back of the church."

This kind woman mothered her as the nuns of her childhood had. Claire didn't want to lose contact with Sister Georgette, as she had with Lucille. "May I come back, before I return to the States, and visit you?"

"You are always welcome here." She sat next to Claire. "Before you leave, may I give you a blessing?"

Tears threatened, but Claire bowed her head and held her hand.

Sister draped the rosary hanging from her belt over their hands and whispered in French. A ray of sunlight poured over them. Warmth drenched Claire. She had not felt this comforted since David's death. She hoped she was healing.

But the memory of the day she arrived at her mother's empty house clawed at her. Pain seared her heart, and it was Sister's loving concern for her that had opened a wound Claire hadn't consciously thought about in more than thirty years.

Chapter 16

Balancing the wrapped dog puppet box in one arm and the cookie box in the other, Claire headed through falling snow toward the Christmas market to purchase more cookies. Lured by a display of grapevine wreaths decorated with miniature birds made of wine corks, she wished she had brought a bigger suitcase.

A group of parents and children swarmed a carousel, and moms and dads helped their kids hop onto the magical creatures. Santa, pulling a donkey wearing a red-leather harness decorated with silver bells, jingled his way through the crowds.

Attracted by the bright, hand-painted ornaments glittering from a stall overflowing with glass icicles, bells, and angels, Claire wandered down a quieter lane. As she stood before a grouping of hand-sewn, felt gingerbread men, storks, and hearts, a memory she'd held tightly in her heart unspooled.

Disoriented and a bit dizzy, she collapsed onto a nearby bench, hugging the puppet and cookies to her.

The scent of pine pulled her to her boarding school in Vermont. The laughter and chatter of girls erupted around her. She had organized an ornament-making day, and all the girls sewed ornaments out of felt, fabric, and ribbon scraps for the school, convent, and church Christmas trees. Claire embroidered silver sequins outlining a white dove's wing, stitched orange glass beads around a goldfish's tail, and gathered lace for a bespectacled mouse's collar. Each of the nuns had a favorite, and the girls embroidered the nuns' names on the back of their chosen ornament.

Spotting a tan and black felt dog kindled a memory of Claire's favorite ornament, a pink poodle on which she'd sewn pink pompoms at its ankles, ears, and tip of its tail. She'd attached a string of rhinestones for a leash and circled them around the dog's neck as a collar. She fashioned the dog after her mother's favorite brooch. Claire had been so proud of the creation, she thought that if she gave the ornament to her mother for Christmas, her mother would love it and love her for making it.

During Thanksgiving weekend, Claire wrote a letter to her mother asking for permission to come home for Christmas. Her mother sent her written permission to Mother Superior. The nuns begged her to remain with them, but Claire convinced them, claiming she was sixteen, nearly an adult and old enough to make the trip on her own. She was so proud of the ornament, she cradled it in her lap the entire bus ride to Connecticut.

When Claire arrived, there were no carols, no tree, no lights. Her mother ordered in Chinese food for dinner. Claire attempted conversation as they ate, but her mother responded only with, 'yes' and 'no.' When they finished dinner, her mother went to bed.

Some Christmas Eve, thought Claire. She stayed up watching and crying all the way through, *It's a Wonderful Life*. But She was determined to have a nice holiday, so she got up early to cook breakfast, but all she found in the kitchen was instant coffee and seven TV dinners stacked in the freezer. No milk, no bread, no orange juice. She made coffee and poured herself a cup, but it was terrible without cream. Her mother didn't even have sugar or Coffee mate.

Mother came downstairs at ten, turned on the TV, and lit up a cigarette. Claire ran and got her coffee, and, when she returned, Mother dug into her robe pocket, pulled out a check, and slid it across the coffee table.

Claire assumed it was her Christmas gift and thanked her. She lovingly presented her beautifully wrapped poodle.

Mother didn't even look at it. She pulled off the paper, said, "Nice," and tossed the poodle on the coffee table next to her ashtray.

Claire remembered Sister Francine clapping in delight when she saw the poodle, and Claire now understood that the nuns tried to dissuade her from coming because they were trying to protect her from her own mother. She missed them as much as they said they would miss her, so she decided to return to the convent the next morning. When she was packing to leave, she found the poodle, covered in cigarette ashes, in the garbage. Mother hadn't even waited to throw it away until Claire left.

Something inside Claire shifted. She no longer wanted her mother's love. She wanted the truth.

She waited until Mother got up and sat on the couch. She wore a pin-striped navy suit, a white silk blouse with a bow tied at the neck, stockings, and heels. Her poodle brooch twinkled from the lapel of her jacket. She pressed her knees together and tugged her skirt to cover them. Claire wondered if she was going to the office—the day after Christmas.

Claire put a cup of coffee on the table in front of her mother, placed the ash-covered poodle ornament next to it, and sat opposite her.

Mother just sat there, staring at the ashtray. Her cheeks were flaccid, her hair streaked with gray, her hands riddled with age spots, as if youth had never graced her.

Claire dragged her fingernails across the couch cushion. "Would you look at me, please?"

Mother shook out a cigarette, lit it, inhaled, and gazed at Claire with half-opened eyes, like she was trying not to notice her daughter—a smudge on the décor.

Anger pulsed through Claire, giving her courage. 'Why do you hate me?"

"Because I chose to have you." A smile wavered.

Her answer dizzied Claire. Was her mother happy, or angry, or smug for having chosen to have her, or for hating her?

Mother flicked the lighter open and closed, open and closed, open and closed. "When I gave birth to you, I lost everyone else in my life."

Although she had expected her mother to deny her hatred, Claire wasn't surprised. She was angry and hurt, but she was calmer than her mother was, which made her brave.

If she couldn't have her mother's love, she wanted the whole truth.

"Who is everyone else?"

"My parents. They kicked me out. Told me if I didn't give the baby up for adoption, they'd disown me.' She drew deeply on her cigarette, exhaled smoke, and with nonchalance said, "So, I disowned them first." She flicked ashes in the tray.

Her reply snuffed Claire's anger. "How could they not want their daughter and grandchild?"

Cold as frost, she replied, "To my parents, what other people thought was more important to them than their daughter."

Compassion warmed Claire's heart. "You must have felt very alone."

"Alone was better than their constant judgment and criticism." Her heavy-lidded eyes dulled.

The realization that her mother treated Claire the way her parents had treated her rolled through Claire, fueling the tangle of anger and compassion. But her quest for understanding burst through. "What about my father?"

"Everything was beautiful until you arrived." Her eyes sparkled for a second—Claire thought in memory of him—and then her eyes darkened. She was so quick to answer it seemed to Claire she had wanted to tell the tale for years. "Two days after you were born, he said he wasn't having any fun. The reality of caring for you was too much for him. He went out that night to get a pizza and didn't return. I never heard from him again."

Claire couldn't imagine abandoning a mother and infant. "How terrible. Did no one else know what happened to him?"

Mother dropped her head, resting her chin on her chest. And at that moment Claire realized how despairing and unloved she must have felt. She wanted to comfort her mother, but the woman was as rigid as she was cold. If Claire got close, her mother might shatter like a piece of glass, or worse, stop talking.

"He was from Canada, and I imagine he fled across the border."

"Did you report him missing?"

She shook her head. "I didn't want him back. If he left me once, he'd do it again."

Claire felt like she'd been kicked in the stomach. Neither of her parents had wanted her. She'd let that sink in later. She wanted the whole story, now. "But how did you support us?"

Mother sat back, taking a deep drag on her cigarette and shot the smoke out toward the ceiling. "He left a few thousand dollars on the dresser—he could afford it—he was a musician. When that ran out, I took in typing jobs until I could afford a babysitter."

"You blame me for losing everyone in your life." Claire thought that would have pricked some emotion, but her mother just gave a half smile.

"I was happy before you came along."

Claire didn't let that sting for a second. "How could you be happy with people who controlled and abandoned you?"

Mother stared at a place far away, beyond Claire.

She wasn't going to let her mother ignore her. "You could have given me up for adoption." She raised her voice. "Why didn't you?"

"I wanted to defy my parents. I'd gone to college while living at home, working part time, and taking care of them. I'd done everything that was expected of me. When they threatened to disown me, I wanted to hurt them, show them what if felt like to be ignored, as they had ignored me, my dreams, my hopes."

"So you used me to spite them."

"Yes."

Claire's voice erupted before she had time to think. "You didn't want me."

"No."

Claire's fingers tingled with cold. She had cushioned her heart with all the kindness the Sisters had shown her. But her mother's malice chipped away at Claire's heart like a pecking bird. Try as her mother might, Claire would never allow her to destroy the Sisters' love that Claire secreted in her heart.

She wanted her mother to know what being hated felt like. "Giving birth to me was a big price to pay for getting rid of all those losers—losers who you say made you happy."

Mother's lips opened, but no words nor smoke escaped her gaping mouth.

Claire stood. "Just think, if you'd had the courage to leave them on your own, you wouldn't have needed me as your pathetic excuse."

The ashes on her mother's cigarette dropped onto her lap.

A sharp taste flushed Claire's mouth. "I'm returning to the convent this afternoon. I don't want to be near anyone who hates me." She picked up the poodle and shook the ashes into her mother's coffee. "You're no better than your parents. You are as selfish and cold to me as they were to you."

Claire longed to say she understood why her father left her mother, but she knew in her heart she couldn't be that cruel. She tucked the poodle in her pocket and picked up her suitcase. Her mother wouldn't look at her, so Claire figured that at least she had shamed her. She voiced the promise she made to herself. "For the rest of my life, I will do everything to ensure I never become anything like you."

On the four-hour bus ride back to the convent, Claire forbade herself to cry. Her mother did not deserve Claire's tears. She never wanted to see her mother again. Claire envisioned clipping all the threads of hurt that wound around her heart until she could inhale deeply. Beginning that day she would plan her life without her mother. She took out her embroidery kit and sewed her name on the back of the poodle.

Claire sat squeezing her eyes against the memory, but it blazed in her mind like a Yule log. A group of carolers, wearing red and green berets, strolled to a fountain and began singing in French, something about stars of snow. A chill slid down her back, and she doubled her scarf around her neck. Her memory had been so real, she wasn't sure where she was—in France or Vermont, and Claire knew she needed help. She set her boxes on the bench, pulled out her phone, and called Marti.

When she answered, Claire gasped, "I remembered something."

"Where are you?" Marti asked.

"Sitting on a bench outside the Christmas market." She stamped her cold feet. "It's snowing, I'm freezing, and I sound like a petulant teenager."

"Do you feel safe?"

"Yes, but I don't know if what I remembered is real."

"Tell me."

Without leaving out any detail, Claire reiterated her memory.

When she finished, she was shivering. "It was the last time I saw her and the last thing I said to her. I don't feel guilty about it, nor do I regret it. But now I wonder if it was a strange coincidence that my mother was dead a year later. Why have I never wondered if she committed suicide?"

She wiped snow from her pants and hunched over her knees. "Oh, Marti, in my effort to not be anything like my mother, I may have overdone it. Was that encounter what made me fear becoming a mother? Was I so committed to being nothing like her that I avoided having children? Why did I just remember this?"

"You must have been terribly, terribly hurt, Claire. And the pain that altercation caused can take a whole lifetime to heal. The repercussions of that confrontation have been reverberating throughout your life. Often, we forget things to protect ourselves. And we can only see things as they really are when we're strong enough and ready to accept them." Her voice was low and comforting. "Like now."

Claire let out a grunt. "I'm glad the bitch died before the next Christmas." She pressed her fingers to her mouth to stop her quivering lips. "Oh, God, that's a terrible thing to say, but I am glad she's dead. I'm a terrible, terrible person. I hate my own mother." Her arms felt tired and limp and useless.

Marti whispered, "You're not terrible. I'm glad too. You deserved a much more loving mother than the one you had."

"Is that why I wasn't honest with David, because I wasn't ready to remember my promise of not being like my mother?"

"You didn't remember that moment until now, so I think that might be true."

Twilight was descending and the lights on the trees and buildings sparkled against an ink-blue sky. Strands of white lights zig-zagged between the buildings' roofs, making a star-studded ceiling above Claire. "It's magical, here. Strange, I've been feeling miserable, but now I'm feeling better."

"That's good. Sometimes when you let emotions out, you feel better, even though expressing emotions can be painful."

"I see. Okay, that's enough memory time. Let's change the subject. I wish you were here."

"No wiggling away so fast. One more question. Do you know if your mother was ever diagnosed with a mental illness?"

"I don't even know how she died."

"I'm no psychiatrist, but I think your mother had something seriously wrong. What she did was cruel, and not something a normal mother would do."

"So, her behavior had nothing to do with me or the poodle?"

"It could be she was severely depressed. But that's not an excuse for how she treated you. She should have sought help to enable her to be a good mother."

"I get it. Now changing the subject, again—"

"Not yet. Why didn't you ever mention how neglectful your mother was?"

As if a church bell rang, something resounded low in Claire, but she couldn't identify it. A fluttering sensation moved across her heart. She searched her memory...neglect...why did she have such a physical reaction to that word? "Was her behavior neglectful?"

"Absolutely. She knew you were coming to visit. She made no preparations for Christmas, which was bad enough, but no food? What would you do for your child for Christmas?"

"I'd decorate everything in sight. I'd cook up a storm. I'd take her to the Christmas parade. We would make cookies and crafts together."

"Exactly."

A family with six laughing children ran across the square and lined up at a steaming copper vat, wafting the scent of cinnamon and sugar across the market. The dad paid and the mom bestowed a candied apple to each child, from the smallest to the tallest.

"I guess I never realized how un-nurturing my mother was."

"That's a lot of sadness to mourn."

"Which will take time. Okay, I got it. How are you and Stephen? Are your patients keeping you overly busy? And is Stephen knee-deep in sawdust?"

"I'm very busy, but I'm glad I can help my patients. I love my work. You know, many people have sad memories about the holidays, like you."

"Really?"

"Really. Patients come in with flu-like symptoms and then talk about all the stress of the holidays."

"Wow, that's not good."

"No. But talking seems to help them. And Stephen's deep in the Christmas spirit because he's been working on so many wooden toys. Can you believe someone requested he carve a banana slug? He's an unofficial Santa's elf. Have you spoken to Gilbert again?"

"I'm on my way back to the hotel. I'll call him from there."

"Keep allowing those memories, Claire. I'm sure it will be difficult at times, but you're very close to uncovering deep things that have frightened you. I've got to go. Call me later."

"Thanks, I will." Claire stuffed her cell in her pocket and pulled on her gloves. She wished she'd kept that adorable poodle. Maybe when she returned, she'd visit the convent and see if any of the Sisters were still there. She would thank them for mothering her.

She plucked up the box of Sister Georgette's cookies. Her mother could have given her up for adoption, but instead, she took her to the convent. Claire wished she had thanked her mother. It was the only good thing she had ever done for her.

CHAPTER 17

Three messages from Gilbert awaited Claire when she arrived at her hotel room. She put her packages in the closet, washed her face, and retrieved the wine and cheese from the minifridge. The housekeeper had carefully wrapped the cheese and corked the wine, and Claire opened both.

At least Gilbert wanted to talk to her. What did she want to happen? She poured the wine, filling the glass. She wanted to know why David hadn't told her about Luca, but she didn't think Gilbert would know the answer to that question. Perhaps he could tell her more about how David behaved with Luca and that would give her some clues. But she knew David had been loving and kind and gentle and fun. And those actions wouldn't give her an explanation.

She ate a piece of cheese and opened the drapes. A family played together in the courtyard, two small children and a mom making angels in the snow. Part of Claire longed to have shared a loving family with David, yet another darker part of her was terrified, but of what, she wasn't certain. She didn't want to be anything like her mother, but there was something else that frightened her. She knew the fear emanated from her mother, but why would her mother's coldness cause Claire to be frightened of having children herself? Claire didn't know how to be a mother, but David would have helped her figure it out.

She sipped the wine, noticing the faint fragrance of an unfamiliar fruit—it wasn't citrus, a little bit plummy—lychee, that was it. She raised her glass to the photo of David that she'd placed on the bedside table.

Her appreciation of him turned to sadness. She wanted to meet Luca but was afraid his resemblance to David would bring tears. And she didn't want to cry in front of the boy.

If Gilbert didn't want her to meet Luca, how would she feel? She massaged her neck as she paced. Left out. Alienated. Even if Luca wasn't her child, he was David's, and she wanted to meet him, even if she cried her eyes out. She'd just have to keep it together and wait to have a melt down until after her visit. She closed the drapes.

After another fortifying sip of wine, she dialed his number.

"Allô?" Gilbert's voice was urgent.

"It's Claire. I'm sorry—"

"I was so worried. Are you okay?"

"Yes, I'm sorry. I was in such a state of shock, I didn't know what I was doing. I'm sorry I worried you."

"It's okay. You are feeling better now?" A dog barked in the background and Gilbert shushed him.

After finding the photo, she'd thought she'd never be the same again, and after learning David knew about Luca, she was devastated, confused, exhausted; but she didn't want to further worry Gilbert. "Yes. Were you able to read the information I gave you?"

"Yes! From the bottom of my heart, I thank you. We have an appointment tomorrow morning for Luca to be tested."

The splinter of worry she'd carried in her heart dissolved. "I am so glad."

"Claire..." A song played in Gilbert's background, and she recognized the words, *Petit Papa Noël*. He cleared his throat. "I don't think we should tell Luca about David's...passing now."

How would they ever tell Luca about David's death? "I understand. I am so sorry for him losing his mother and David."

"I am too, but Luca is resilient and a joyful child. I always reward him after a medical visit, and he would like to go to Strasbourg for a boat ride to view Christmas lights. Would you like to join us?"

Words stuck in her throat. She wanted to yell yes, but darkness encroached, squelching her words. She squeezed her eyes and opened them, searching for something to focus on. The gilt-framed photo of Frédéric Bartholdi had occupied the same place on the wall when she and David honeymooned here, inspiring them to visit his home and view his models for his Statue of Liberty.

"Claire? Are you there?"

She shook her head to free herself of memories. "Yes. I..."

"Are you worried you will become upset?"

"How did you know that?"

"I would feel the same. If we meet at your hotel, I'll bring the envelope for you. After I introduce you, you can excuse yourself to take the envelope to your room, which will give you time to collect yourself. If it's not enough time, I will send Luca to speak to the owner about a wine delivery. We will wait. Is that an okay plan?"

She laughed. "You are so very kind and thoughtful, Gilbert. Yes. I think that is a very good plan. Does Luca speak English?"

"Better than I do. We will arrive at ten, if that is good?"

"Yes. Of course." She drummed her fingers on the glass. "Gilbert?"

"Oui?"

She took a long swallow of wine. "Did David see Luca every time he visited the winery?"

"Yes." His voice was soft, as if the word might bruise her.

"Luca must miss him very much."

"He does. He asked about David nearly every day before...Sophie passed."

Something twisted in Claire. The poor child was still grieving for his mother. This was no time to give him another shock.

"Does Luca know David was married...not to Sophie, but to me?"

"No."

"But when he learns the truth, he'll know we lied to him." Her heartbeat raced.

"If he knows you are David's wife, he will ask you about him. Better he does not know that David passed. Luca has been mourning his maman for the past year. The anniversary of her death is Christmas Eve. I don't know how much more he can take. And I cannot bear to see the anguish on his face, again."

Claire ran her hands over the shiny and rough damask fabric of the armchair. She had done plenty of lying in her life, but never to a child. She couldn't imagine herself telling a child whose mother had died that his father was also dead.

"I think it best we do not tell him now. Let him get to know you as a friend I met at the hotel who is interested in wine. That is not such a big lie."

She massaged her thumb. "You know what is best for Luca."

"Bien, à demain, sorry, until tomorrow."

She inhaled and forced her lips around the words. "Bien, à demain."

She stared out the window, trying to fathom how David could laugh and play with his son and leave him. And not share Luca with her. Why did David agree to something that must have brought him such joy, yet also pain? Visiting Luca must have filled his heart with joy to overflowing yet torn his heart every time he left.

Claire wanted to call Marti, but due to the time difference she didn't want to interrupt her work with her patients. Texting her would disrupt her day, and she didn't want to infringe on her clinic time. Would Marti think not telling Luca about David's death was okay? She turned out the lights and sat on the couch opposite the window, Elvis crying about a blue Christmas faintly echoing in the courtyard.

Sister Georgette's kitchen had so warmed her. She'd not thought about Lucille and Carmine in such a long time, yet the memory brought tears and longing and regret. She would try to reconnect with them when she returned. Lucille had been warmer to her in one day than her mother had been in Claire's entire lifetime. And she imagined Carmine as the dad she never had.

Had Claire's mother's mother been cold to her daughter? Except when Claire confronted her on Christmas, her mother never spoke of her parents, and Claire never met them. Until that conversation, she hadn't known she had grandparents. She'd searched for photographs of her grandparents in her mother's papers but not found any photos, documents, mementos, souvenirs. It seemed her mother had not wanted to leave so much as her footprint on life.

Had her mother spent her childhood in the same convent Claire had? She punched the couch cushion. She knew trying to figure out her mother was fruitless, and wasting thoughts on her mother prevented Claire from understanding herself. But maybe exploring her mother's actions would be the beginning of facing her own fears.

Snowflakes slid down the window and piled up on the ledge. There was a very dark place in Claire's mind, which she was afraid to explore, but even if she had the courage to face it, she didn't know how to get there. She hoped she'd find a way to enter and control that darkness.

First, she had to muster the courage to meet Luca.

CHAPTER 18

Dawn's pink, then violet, then golden light bathed the courtyard. Snow covered everything like a layer of sparkling icing. The silence was as blissful as a cup of hot chocolate. Despite spending the night staring out the window, searching her childhood memories, Claire had no deeper insight into her mother.

In her heart, she knew she was nothing like her mother. Claire had made certain of that because her mother was not liked by anyone. Even as a child, when neighbors saw them walking down the sidewalk, they crossed the street. In church, she and her mother often sat alone in the pew, not joined even by members of the clergy.

While her mother had no confidants, Claire befriended nearly every girl at boarding school. Her mother was an attorney, obsessed with words. Claire was a designer, obsessed with colorful fabrics, sensual textures, and the mechanics of a built-in life preserver. Her mother never cooked. Once David taught her how, they cooked together most every meal, and David complimented her on *having the knack.*

She guessed her knack came from sitting in front of the kitchen fireplace while the nuns whipped up hearty stews and wholesome desserts. They often involved her in sifting and stirring and chopping, although, unlike Sister Georgette, none of them offered her a teacup of brandy. A warm fondness filling her heart made her promise herself to pay Sister Georgette another visit before she returned home.

Brenda Lee's *Rockin' Around the Christmas Tree* erupted in the courtyard and pushed Claire to get ready to meet her husband's son. She closed the drapes. Eyeing the beribboned package holding the dog-puppet, she decided to save it for another day. If the meeting didn't go well, she could use delivering the gift as an excuse to see him again.

She picked up the box of Sister Georgette's cookies and wished she'd bought two more, but she was glad she had one to give Gilbert. She'd have something to hold onto. Omitting the truth wasn't exactly lying to Luca, but her agreement with Gilbert still bothered her. The boy had lost so much, and she didn't want to worsen his grief with news of his father's death, as Gilbert had cautioned her. But would Luca feel betrayed when they finally told him? She didn't know how children think, much less how they process grief. She was not Luca's mother, and she needed to honor Gilbert's decision.

At the top of the steps, Claire clutched the cookie box and gazed down at her husband's son. Standing below the chandelier, Gilbert held Luca's hand. Both sported red berets. Luca's smile warmed her like Sister Georgette's kitchen.

Lured by his smile, she descended.

As she reached the last step, Gilbert removed his cap. "Claire, may I present my son, Luca?"

Luca whipped off his cap and gave a quick bow. "I am enchanté to meet you Madame Claire." His brown eyes and curls glowed against his white parka.

Her heart battered her ribs. His accent was sweet, like syrup on crêpes. "I am enchanté to meet *you*, Luca." She descended the last step and extended her hand to shake.

He lightly held her fingers and kissed them, his eyes sparkling.

"You are a very charming gentleman." Her voice cracked. "And you speak English so well."

Luca's dimples intensified his dazzling smile. "You are very pretty, like Papa David said."

Her legs weakened. She stepped back, dropped the box of cookies, reached for the balustrade, and lowered herself onto the third step. The hotel lobby pressed around her.

Gilbert rushed to her, gripped her elbow. "Are you feeling unwell?" Lines creased his forehead.

"You said he didn't know," she whispered.

The pain in his eyes answered her. He hadn't known Luca knew about her.

She wiped perspiration from her upper lip. Her legs stretched over the steps before her, like a toddler's. "Just a bit dizzy. I guess I should have had a bigger breakfast."

Gilbert picked up the cookie box and placed it on the step beside her. "Can I get you a glass of water?"

"No. I'm fine. Just need a minute."

Worrying his hat, Luca looked up at her. His eyes held pure innocence. "You are Papa David's wife."

She glanced at Gilbert, but he closed his eyes. She was on her own. Something hard, like a chunk of ice, sat in her throat.

Luca's smile was broad, proud.

She was sure Gilbert told her Luca didn't know David was married. She swallowed against the lump. "Did..." she struggled to find words. "Did your Papa David tell you about me?"

"He showed me pictures of you, and your maillots, on his mobile." Luca climbed the first two steps until he was face-to-face with her. "Where is Papa David?"

Gilbert's mouth contorted, pressing against emotions more than words, Claire suspected. He put his hand on his son's shoulder.

Claire didn't care what she'd promised Gilbert—she owed David's son the truth. If she lied, it would only be worse for Luca later. A pressure built in her. She raised an eyebrow to Gilbert, and he nodded.

Putting her arm around Luca, she inhaled his little boy scent of brioche and Nutella. No matter how this beautiful boy came into her life, he was a part of David, and she cherished them both.

Gilbert stood above them, his face awash in sorrow, his fist pressing against his mouth.

She pulled Luca up onto her lap and swallowed against the hard thing in her throat. "David hasn't visited in a long time, has he?"

Luca shook his head. "I hope he is not buying our competitors' wines."

Gilbert let go of a sob-laugh.

David would have found Luca's comment sad-funny as well.

"He would have visited you if he could..." Claire hugged Luca to her; stroked his unruly curls from his eyes; cupped his cheek. "But he couldn't...because he passed away." She held him gently, like he might break, giving him the freedom to flee if he wished.

"Oh... Like Maman." He leaned his head against her shoulder and let out a long, shuddering sigh. "When did he die?"

Claire exchanged a worried glance with Gilbert. She didn't know why David had told Luca about her but not her about Luca. A sense of betrayal slid through her. She pushed her own feelings aside. She had to support this boy in his grief, and she would not lie. She would be strong for Luca.

She held him close and spoke softly. "Last year in September—right before he was going to visit you. I didn't know about you then, otherwise I would have come to tell you much sooner."

Luca searched her eyes, making Claire glad she'd been honest with him, even if Gilbert was angry with her. "How did he die?"

"His heart stopped working. It was very sudden."

"Oh." He gently kicked his legs, like he was ridding himself of stress. "I am glad he was not sick for a long time, like Maman. Do you think he is in heaven with her?"

"Yes, I believe they are both in heaven."

He wrapped his arms around her neck. "Don't cry, Madame Claire." He patted her back.

She held him, felt the weight of him, felt him sigh and inhale a shaky breath. A warmth she'd never known bloomed in her, enabling her to comfort Luca, and at the same time realizing he comforted her—like giant arms cradled and warmed and protected them both. The feeling was holy, like an aura surrounding them. She understood now, the paintings of the Virgin Mary and her child. Motherhood was holy. She basked in the sacredness of holding and comforting David's son, never wanting the moment to end, knowing she would love and protect this child for the rest of her life.

She felt sorry for her mother, then, never knowing the comfort Claire could have given her. Sister Georgette was right. Her mother had missed out on loving her beautiful daughter. And Claire was grateful beyond imagination that she had this opportunity to love David's beautiful son.

Luca straightened. "You must miss him beaucoup...much. And you must be very sad." He looked up at Gilbert. "Are you sad, too, Onc?"

Gilbert nodded. "David was my very good friend." He dragged his fist across his mouth.

She imagined he was suppressing his pain. Claire had been so concerned about Luca she hadn't grasped Gilbert's loss, and she longed to help him recover from his grief. David had given Gilbert's sister what she desired most in life. Gilbert must have loved David very much for not only his generosity, but also for giving them both a son.

Luca hugged Claire. "I am sad not to see Papa David anymore, but I am glad he sent you to us. He told us many stories about your...maillots?"

"Swimsuits." Claire squeezed Luca and held on for dear life, trying not to cry. She breathed slowly until she calmed. "I am very glad to be with you. Your Papa David loved you so, so very much."

Luca let out a long sigh and stood, looking up at Gilbert and then Claire. "Do you want to go with us to Strasbourg? Papa David loved the city. It is very pretty, and the trip will help us feel less sad."

The heaviness in Claire drained. "How do *you* feel, Luca?"

He rubbed his hand in circles on his chest. "It hurts here, but I know it is because I am sad and missing my maman *and* papa." He examined his fingers like a toy he'd never seen. "But Papa David told me that he would always be in my heart." He pressed his fingers on his chest. "And I feel him right here, right now." He tilted his head; his face was serious. "Do you feel him in your heart?"

Claire nodded. "Always."

"Then let us take Papa David with us to Strasbourg."

His simple logic tugged a smile from her. "He would like that very much."

Gilbert bent down and lifted Luca, settling the boy on his shoulders. "Ready?"

"Allons-y!" Luca looked down at Claire. "That means, let us go!" His excited voice possessed David's enthusiasm and joy.

Gilbert helped Claire stand and gave her the envelope. She picked up the box of cookies and walked to the front desk.

Madame Justine wiped her eyes and replaced her glasses. "Forgive me for listening, but I am so very sorry about Monsieur David," she whispered.

"Thank you." Claire held out the envelope. "Would you have someone put this in my room please?"

"I will do it, myself."

Claire didn't care that Madame Justine probably thought David had been unfaithful to her. What other people thought just didn't matter. What mattered now was Luca. She didn't know how she'd do it, but she would help him heal. And a couple of cookies could help them all feel a bit better for a few moments.

She walked out into the day, her heart heavy. Why did David not tell her about Luca, but he told Luca about her?

CHAPTER 19

Luca slid down from Gilbert's shoulders and took her hand, leading her to a red SUV. She could have laughed at the brand, a Citroën, the type of car she and David had bought used—falling apart, really—for touring Europe on their honeymoon. Gilbert took the scenic Wine Route toward Strasbourg.

Questions pounded in her head. Her marriage was not the trusting relationship she'd thought it was. David hadn't trusted her to discuss his becoming a donor much less tell her about Luca. Did he not talk to her for fear she'd object, and he wanted a child so badly he'd chosen not to risk telling her? Did having a son have anything to do with not making a will? Claire remembered discussing making wills, but it was one of those things she hadn't gotten around to, and neither had David. It was unlike him not to have all his records up-to-date. She was the one who often had the overdrawn checking account, never him.

A burning sensation brushed the edges of her throat. But if he had drawn up a will, wouldn't he have included a provision for Luca, or at least set up a trust for his college education? Did David fear her discovering Luca if he had a will?

David could have written a will and given it to his attorney with instructions not to reveal it to Claire until his death. David should have left instructions for an executor to set up a trust for Luca—even if was a shock to Claire, at least she would have known.

As the road curved, sunlight sparkled on the snow-covered mountains, blinding her. She didn't want to admit the truth, but it was clear: David didn't want her to know about Luca, even in death. A sound like cracking ice broke through every belief she held about her marriage. She had thought they were soulmates. She believed their marriage was based on trust and honesty. The reality was they were mates who kept secrets for the sake of their marriage.

The question of why David told Luca about her and not her about Luca burned a hole in her heart. Whatever the reason, the look of love for his Papa David on Luca's face was worth every bit of pain and confusion Claire endured.

Luca's voice brought her back from her thoughts to the car. "Those mountains—" he pointed, "they are the Vosges. And that castle? Built in the thirteenth century. I hope you have time to visit Kaysersberg. I take you, happily. In these vineyards...Riesling grapes."

"How are you so young and knowledgeable?" Claire asked.

"I am not so young, I am almost eight." He sat back. "Maman taught me."

Claire checked Gilbert's face. A mixture of, what she thought were, humor, pride, and grief tugged at his eyes.

"But Onc teaches me, now."

"Why do you call Gilbert, Onc?"

Luca's giggles bounced like bubbles. "When I learn to talk, I could not say the "cle" sound in oncle, the French word for uncle, so I called him Onc, with a long O."

Claire repeated, "Onc."

"Bien." Luca clapped and turned. "Onc is not difficult to say. Try to say Riquewhir!"

Claire closed her eyes, fearing the word would bring tears. "What did Papa David tell you about me?"

"That you are very pretty—he was right. You travel much to India and China, is that right?"

She nodded. "I did."

"Not anymore?" He leaned forward to peer at her between the seats.

"No...I was fired." She laughed. It *was* funny when she thought about it, now that there was no danger of the model being hurt.

"Fired is meaning no job?"

"That is correct. My invention...well...it blew up while the model was wearing the bathing suit, and she was very frightened—but she wasn't hurt, and my boss fired me." A trill of laughter convulsed her, and she bent over her knees, giving into a fit of giggles.

Gilbert patted her shoulder. "Are you okay?"

Trying to control her laughing, she wiped away tears. "I was pretty upset when it happened, very disappointed actually, but now, it's pretty funny. The invention kept pumping air and wouldn't stop. The tubing swelled to the size of a car tire, and I had to destroy the contraption."

"Being fired is not a good thing, is it?" Luca asked.

"No, it's not a good thing, Luca. But I think I tried way too hard, and it is best that the invention didn't work because if it had, I wouldn't have met you and Onc." She tapped her finger on Luca's nose. "And I'm very glad to be here with you both, now."

"Bien." Luca's smile reassured her.

So what if she lost a job of twenty-three years? The court would settle David's estate after the holidays. She didn't need to worry about finding a new job for a month. Tightness crept up her spine. David should have included Luca in his will. Now that she knew about Luca, she had to inform the attorney and set up a trust for Luca. But when she informed the court that David had a son, the estate would be sent to probate court again, blocking money she needed for another year.

The tightness spread across her shoulders. Who would hire a fifty-year-old woman who'd been fired? She couldn't even collect unemployment. How would she pay for health insurance? And the taxes on the house? And the airfare to France she'd charged? She shook herself and focused on appreciating the stunning scenery.

Gilbert turned on the radio, and Nat King Cole crooned his chestnut song.

Luca sang along and Gilbert joined him.

"Why are all the Christmas songs American? Surely there are French carols?"

"The Christmas markets, restaurants, hotels, and radio stations play American songs because they are universally recognized and popular. The French carols are played in churches and in homes." Gilbert beat his thumbs against the steering wheel in time with the music.

"We have French words to some of the same carols," said Luca. "Guess which one this is, Mon beau sapin, mon beau sapin—" he sang

"Oh Christmas Tree?"

Luca slapped the car seat. "You are a very fast learner."

She didn't tell him she recognized the song from the melody rather than the words.

As they passed the sign for Riquewhir, a miasma of emotions churned in her. Fear had disabled her from experiencing this joy with David. She deeply regretted preventing him from being a full-time, well-loved father, yet at the same time, anger gnawed at him for keeping the joy of loving this child a secret. She chewed at her chapped lip. Why?

"We go to a Winstub—wine bar." Luca skipped ahead. An ancient, half-timbered, tilting building decorated in white lights and teddy bears, and silver ornaments claimed a busy corner.

As they entered a cavernous dining room, a cacophony of conversations, clattering dishes, and Burl Ives bellowing *A Holly Jolly Christmas* filled the wood-paneled room. White pine chairs, with hearts carved out of the chairbacks, surrounded tables sporting red-and-white-checked cloths.

Luca followed the hostess and pulled out a chair. "Madame Clair? S'il te plaît."

"Merci." Claire raised her eyebrows at Gilbert who smiled.

Luca sat next to her. "So, you speak French!"

"Only a few words."

Gilbert sat at Claire's other side, plucked up her napkin, and placed it on her lap. She was surrounded by two charming French gentlemen.

Afternoon light streamed through arched stained-glass windows and sparkled in Luca's eyes. "Then I teach you. I taught Papa David, and he taught me English. So, I teach you French."

David had pretended not to be fluent in French to give his son the opportunity to teach him. She could have sobbed at David's kindness, his thoughtfulness, his unselfish love. But why not share this with her? Did he not trust her to accept his donorship? Did he fear she'd divorce him? Before she'd met Luca she might not have been so understanding of David's decision. Their marriage was based in *some* trust, but their trust only went so far, on both sides.

Gilbert patted her arm. "Claire may not want to learn."

Luca frowned. "You like me to teach you?"

"Oui!"

"Bon. That means, good."

"Bon."

"See? You learn very fast."

She would never tire of his bubbling giggles, so vibrant and joyous. He must have inherited his laugh from Sophie, for David's laughter was much deeper. Claire opened the menu and held it close to her face. She'd do anything to have David here with her, delighting in this beautiful child. The more she knew of Luca, the angrier she grew at herself for being afraid, and not giving David the happiness he deserved. He should be here with his son. This joy should be his, not hers.

"Onc! We have Flammkuchen?" Luca leaned close to Claire. "Sounds terrible—like it will catch you on fire," he snatched her sleeve, "but it is like pizza, only better, with French cheese." He let go of her and smiled.

Her laughter burst.

"But she might wish the specialty, choucroute?" Gilbert asked.

"Oh, no. No, no, no. The flaming pizza sounds perfect."

Luca slapped his leg. "I knew it. Americans love French pizza."

Gilbert laughed with her and ordered wine, salads, and Flammkuchen.

Luca lifted the saltshaker. "Le sel."

She was grateful he started with a word she remembered. "Le sel."

Gilbert lifted his napkin.

Luca whispered, "La serviette."

Claire repeated words until the food arrived. Then she learned words of appreciation, like magnifique and délicieux. Wanting no more lessons, she longed to change the conversation. "What did you ask Santa for?"

Luca's face crumpled. He dropped his fork. Gilbert patted her hand and rubbed Luca's back.

What had she done? "I'm so sorry. American children—"

"It's all right. Just a bad memory, eh, Luca?"

He nodded fiercely, as if the action would stop his tears. Gilbert pulled him onto his lap and hugged him. Luca gripped Gilbert's shirt and buried his face between Gilbert's shoulder and chin.

Claire's heartbeat thundered. How could she make this better if she didn't know what she'd done? Her heart squeezed. She was a terrible person to hurt this child. She *would* have been a terrible mother. She should leave. She watched Gilbert, figuring it was grief etching deep lines on either side of his mouth and clamping his jaw tight, like a lock, as he rubbed circles on Luca's back. Why had she brought up Santa? Was he not part of French Christmas? She'd seen plenty of them in the markets. Whatever the reason, she was sorely lacking in mothering skills.

Luca quieted. Gilbert kissed his forehead and handed him a handkerchief. Luca blew his nose. Gilbert whispered, "Would you like to tell Claire about your maman?"

Luca nodded and looked at Claire. She thought her heart would cleave, witnessing the pain afflicting this joyous boy. Although Luca had handled the news of David's death better than she had, she now fully grasped why Gilbert didn't want to tell him. How could she make this better for both of them?

"Last year I wrote a letter to Santa and asked him to make Maman better—she was very sick. But he couldn't do it." His cheeks reddened. "Maman said God couldn't make her better either, so she had to go to heaven and tell God how angry we were. I don't believe in Santa anymore." He kicked his foot out. "And I'm still mad at God. You, Onc?"

"Oui." Gilbert's voice was gruff.

She cleared her throat. "I don't believe in Santa either. I just pretend."

Luca sat up. "You do?"

Claire nodded. "And I've been angry at God many times. I still am."

A quiet calm settled over them like a cloud sent from heaven. Claire wished she knew how to help Luca be happy again. They'd been having so much fun before her Santa mistake.

Luca leaned against Gilbert, breathing deeply. "Onc, can I take the rest of the Flammkuchen home for Remy?"

Claire jumped to change the subject and pretended she didn't know about their dog. "Who is Remy?"

Luca pulled Gilbert's sleeve. "Onc, show her photos. Remy, he is our dog, the best dog in the entire universe."

Claire oohed and aahed over Remy photos, laughing at Remy's foibles, all the while vowing to never hurt Luca again. She would have to figure out a way to help him with his grief like Marti helped her with hers.

Gilbert paid the bill and thanked the waiter. "Ready for a boat ride?"

Claire's hands trembled. She ran a lipstick over her chapped lips, smiled, and gripped Gilbert's elbow. She hoped she had the courage to board the vessel.

Chapter 20

A sleek, glass-roofed pleasure craft bobbed on the river, awaiting them. Claire inhaled a muddy scent. A wariness pricked its way up her spine. She forced herself to concentrate on the festive white lights outlining the boat and reflecting off the water. She longed to know Luca better, and this was what he wanted to do, so she'd do it.

Gilbert and Luca held her hands and guided her up the ramp onto the crowded craft and into a row of seats at the very back.

"Want to sit next to the window?" Luca asked. The window stretched from the seats up to the glass roof, exposing a view of water everywhere.

"Oh, no." She clutched her scarf. "You sit there, please. You can be my guide."

Luca sat next to the window and pointed. "We're going to turn right toward Petite France. If we don't, we'll be swept into the Rhine and out to sea!"

Claire gripped her handbag strap, wishing it were a life preserver. She should have brought her prototype and hoped it worked.

Gilbert placed his hand over hers. "The Rhine is very wide, no danger of being swept to sea. Boys of this age delight in the prospect of danger."

His hand was comforting, and she was glad for its warmth. She pushed out a breath, wishing she could call Marti, but she had to figure things out for herself. Besides, Marti would tell her she was falling in love with Gilbert, just like she told her she was falling in love with David. Good grief, what was she thinking. She'd known the man for less than two days.

"You're a wonderful father."

He shrugged, trying for humility, but he smiled broadly.

Safety instructions in myriad languages crackled over the speakers, a buzzing muddled the English words. Claire pushed her hat from her ears and looked for the safety card airlines provided in the seatback, but there was no pocket. Swiveling her head, she searched for a sign with the universal red cross.

Gilbert's arm encircled her shoulders. "They are saying that life preservers are under our seat cushions, but I can assure you, we will not need them. Should there be a problem in the canals, we could walk in the shallow water and step up onto the seawall."

She took a small breath and forced a smile against her anxiety, but she was also enjoying the weight and warmth and security of his arm. She hoped he'd keep it there.

The vessel's engine whined, and the boat pulled away from the dock and floated down river.

Luca pummeled the seat. She grasped the edge. He jumped up. "That's the...Onc, what is, la Tour du Bourreau?"

"Executioner's Tower."

"Right." Luca laughed. "They tortured people up there! Cool, huh?" He slammed himself back into his seat, shaking her and dislodging Gilbert's arm.

"Cool." She nodded, thinking the boat ride was enough of a torture. Anxiety knotted her stomach. She wished she could ask Gilbert to put his arm back on her shoulder, but that would definitely be too forward.

"The channel will take us around the oldest parts of the city, Petite France and Quartier des Tonneliers—the Coopers' Quarter," Gilbert pointed, "where they made hoops for barrels in the sixteenth century. We have an ancient barrel at the winery, and I imagine it was made there. I'll show it to you."

"I'd like to see it." She'd love to be in the winery rather than on the river. She kept her eyes on the land, focusing on the distant cathedral spire. The boat bounced along turbulent water, and she gripped Gilbert's arm.

"The currents can be rather tricky, due to the channels and locks. The water powered the mills and drew water for the tanneries in the old town." He rubbed his hand along her arm, and it calmed her for a second until a wave broke against the window next to Luca.

She nodded, feeling like an empty-headed puppet. They turned into a narrow passage, bordered on both sides by Tudor-style buildings. A pair of swans glided below a willow tree overhanging the canal. "The swans seem to like it."

"The current churns up food for them."

"Swans mate for life." Why she said that, she did not know. "Sorry, that was an irrelevant, stupid thing to say."

"Not at all irrelevant or stupid." Gilbert released her grip on his arm and patted her hand. "David was my good friend, and he spoke often of you, with great admiration and affection," he whispered. "He has been gone for more than a year, now?"

"A year and almost four months."

"He would want you to be happy." His eyes were more gray than blue, like the sky, but brighter, not ominous. He caressed her fingers.

She'd not been touched in so long, and his hands were gentle and warm and caring. Would David approve of the attraction she felt? She didn't need his approval, even if she thought she did, but she felt disloyal. Desire and guilt tangled in her like a clump of seaweed.

Luca jumped up. "I want to feed the swans." He grabbed the handle of the sliding window and pushed the window open.

Claire grabbed his waist, fearing he might fall out. A chilling breeze seized her. "Can we do that after we get off the boat?" Her voice was high, breathy.

He laughed. "I forgot about this glass cover." He yanked the window closed. "Can we walk back to old town and see the decorations and the big tree in the square, Onc?"

"Would you like that, Claire? After the boat ride, we can take a walk around the old town. It's charming and not far." Gilbert asked.

"Walking? Bien sûr."

"I'm right, you are a very fast learner." Luca's smile brightened the whole boat ride.

She let go of his waist. He sat down and leaned against her, humming *Oh, Christmas Tree*. She put her arm around him, feeling his warmth and joy spread into her.

The boat drifted along a canal where steep-roofed, half-timbered buildings bedecked in white lights, pine boughs, and red ribbons, reflected in the water, now calm as glass. Despite the river, she loved sharing the day with them. She wanted to spend more days with them.

She never thought she'd dread returning to Seattle. She didn't want to. But Marti was counting on her being with them for Christmas...four days away.

CHAPTER 21

Wiping her sweaty hands on her slacks and exhaling the breath she'd held since she'd boarded the boat, she joined hands with Gilbert and Luca. Clouds dimmed the weak December light, hastening dusk. Ancient buildings and tall Christmas trees blinked with lights. They skirted the throngs of people heading for the Christmas market and headed down a snow-dusted hill toward the Ill River.

They strolled along a wide sidewalk running beside a stone embankment that sloped steeply to the river. When they stopped to gaze at the swirling water heading out of town to join the Rhine, Gilbert dropped her hand. "I must find a restroom. Wait here with Luca? I'll be right back."

Before she could speak, Gilbert was jogging up the hill toward the market. She'd made Luca cry in the restaurant. She didn't trust herself to take good care of him, but she would try her best and not say a word about his mom or Santa.

Luca pointed. "Look, that dog looks like Remy!"

Farther down the riverbank, a man threw a ball to a black, brown, and white shaggy dog who leaped to catch it.

Luca laughed. "He's funny. He should be in the circus."

The sound of rushing water grew louder. A mist encircled Claire like a veil. She blinked, trying to focus, but that dark place in her was stirring, taunting her. She'd thought being on the boat was frightening, but why was it that the fear of water threatened to overwhelm her? She shook her shoulders against the prickling running up her back and down her shoulders.

Luca squeezed her hand. "Remy does that with the ball, too."

She squinted, blinking to clear her vision. The dog jumped and arced and snatched the ball in his jaws. Stunned, she cried, "He nearly did a complete flip."

Luca's laughter jingled like sleigh bells.

The dog ran after another ball and leaped. As he came down, he lost his footing and slid. He dropped his ball, yelped. Sliding on all four paws down the stone embankment, he scrambled for his footing, lost his purchase on the steep incline, and fell into the river.

Luca dropped Claire's hand and ran.

"Luca! Stop!" She screamed, racing after him, her feet tripping as she ran on the slippery walkway. "Stop!"

The dog's black head popped up above the water. He barked, but he was already several yards downriver.

Luca's feet pounded, following the dog, calling to him, "Vien ici!"

"Luca, stop!" He's going to go in after that dog. No! Running, she threw her purse away, pulled off her hat, ripped open her coat and pulled off her scarf. The dog bobbed farther away. Luca sped up and ran downriver of the dog. She shrugged off her coat and threw it. "Luca!"

He curved to the left toward a stone wall. A wall where a life ring buoy hung, which she thought Luca was after, but he turned and—she realized in horror—took a running start and threw himself into the water.

Luca's head popped up next to the dog's.

Heart pounding, she sped to the wall and yanked the ring buoy off its hook and shucked off her shoes. She ran to the river's edge, and, gripping the rope loop, tossed the ring into the water near Luca. But the ring landed too far from him.

She took a running start and jumped. Freezing darkness swallowed her. She pulled the buoy rope and surfaced next to the ring, searching for Luca. His white parka glowed beyond her reach; her arms swept toward it. She kicked, flailed, fingers grasping for any part of him. Lungs aching, she kicked, reaching, grasping, scraping against the slippery jacket. Her arms swept the water, her fingers hooked the hood, but it slid from her grasp.

She prayed, *David help me. Help me save your son.*

She lunged and grasped Luca's hood and pulled him to her. Kicking furiously, she pulled the life ring to them, scissoring her legs, again, and again. She gasped for breath. Screamed, "Luca!"

She pulled the life ring under him. "Hold on!"

Luca's legs scrambled; his boots struck her chest, pushing her under. She launched him above her head and kicked with every muscle in her body. Luca was yanked from her hands. Someone must have pulled him out. He was safe.

The life ring's rope slid from her grasping fingers. She gulped air. A dog barked. An icy wave rolled over her. Her legs were so heavy, she couldn't kick. Her arms, spent, useless, trailed above. The unreachable gray sky taunted her. Darkness entrapped her like a pall, dragging her down.

Flurrying bubbles so pretty, sparkling like Christmas lights. The roaring water silenced.

CHAPTER 22

Claire swept her arms before her, moving like a butterfly's wings, scooping water behind her and propelling her forward into a velvet softness. All was calm. All was bright.

She blinked against the brightness. A white room whirled around her as she struggled to focus on something, anything that could bring her onto land, for she was certain she was far away from the real world. But she was alone. If she had died, David would be with her. If she wasn't dead, where was she? Was she dreaming?

Bleeps and blips erupted, louder and more monotonous than the American carols. She wished to hear Bing's *White Christmas.*

As she tried drawing a deep breath, she coughed and spasmed. What happened? Why did she feel as if she was wrapped like a mummy and her lungs were filled with muck? She struggled to sit up.

A hand gentled hers. She squinted, looking for David, but as she focused, she recognized Gilbert's face. She longed to fall into his arms.

He wrapped his strong arms around her. "How do you feel?" Worry creased his forehead and tugged at his, bluer than gray, eyes.

Blissful, now that you're here, she longed to say, but that wasn't appropriate...was it? "Safe," she whispered.

Not loosening his grip on her, Gilbert dropped his head onto her shoulder. "Merci," he whispered and sobbed. His muscular shoulders shook, and she wondered what could have possibly happened to make such a strong man weep. "I'm sorry I left you. I shouldn't have. I was terrified I'd lost you both."

The memory of Luca running along a river toward a dog flashed in her mind.

"Luca!" She lurched. "Where is Luca? Is he safe?" Her body trembled.

Gilbert's head popped up. "He is fine. He's playing with some children in the waiting room." He wiped his face. "Do you know where you are?"

"I'm pretty sure this is a hospital. But why am I here? Why am I shaking?"

"What do you remember?" He pulled the blanket up over her shoulders.

Picturing Luca and the dog, she searched, but only the memory of the Winstub bubbled up. "Flammkuchen. Delicious."

Gilbert laughed.

"I'm starving."

"You don't remember anything after the Winstub?" His normally bright eyes dulled.

Claire wondered if he was sad or in pain. She searched for images, but nothing came to her. "What's wrong?"

"Madame Claire. You're awake!" Luca ran to the side of the bed. The beeping sped up. "Magnifique!"

The beeps tripled. The ache in Claire's heart melted, and she thrummed with joy at his voice. "Luca! Are you all right?"

"I am super fine, Madame Claire!" He kissed her cheek.

She wanted to grasp his little face and smother it with kisses, but she was so tired, she didn't think her fingers would work.

Gilbert pressed her back into the pillows. "Yes, he's fine, thanks to you." He caressed her cheek. "You must rest, now."

White and green uniformed medical people flooded the room. Her eyelids fluttered. She was so tired.

CHAPTER 23

Claire begged for a cup of coffee and a croissant. A nurse smiled at her. "Tout de suite." The medical exam exhausted her. A young doctor told her she'd been unconscious for eighteen hours. No wonder she was starving.

The doctor left and Gilbert and Luca appeared beside Claire's bed in an instant.

"They told me I fell into a river?"

"I saved the dog! And you saved me!"

Gilbert smiled at Luca and tousled his hair.

Images of a dog playing ball alongside the river emerged from her foggy memory. She laughed. "That's impossible. I'm terrified of the water."

"But—"

"Luca, would you please go get some of Sister Georgette's cookies for Claire?"

"Bien sûr." He scooted out the door.

"We bought another box." Gilbert sat next to the bed and held her hand. "The doctor said you might not remember, but you did save Luca's life. You jumped into the river with a life ring—very quick thinking—and pulled him onto the buoy and pushed him toward the embankment where a man pulled Luca out. I was running toward you. But—you went under. The dog bit your sleeve and towed you to his owner, who pulled you out." His eyes glistened. "I am forever indebted to you for saving Luca's life." He kissed her fingers. Tears ran down his cheeks.

She wiped his tears. She wanted to believe him; he had no reason to lie. But that just wasn't possible. "I can't believe it."

"Why?"

Words stuck in her mouth like rocks in mud. Her lips struggled to form the words. She coughed against the taste of muddy water and calmed. "I don't think I can swim."

"But...then...how?" Alarm filled his eyes. "You threw the buoy, and you jumped in after him. Like you knew what you were doing."

Had she? The nuns had insisted she attend water-safety classes, but she didn't remember taking swimming lessons.

The scent of the river made her shudder. She remembered running and grabbing the life ring. And she remembered the first rule of water safety was not to jump in, but to throw the buoy to the victim and tow him in. Was the rope not long enough to reach Luca? Was that why she'd jumped? Had Luca not surfaced?

Luca's dimpled smile beamed up at her. He held out a plate of cookies. "Did Onc invite you to stay with us for Christmas?"

Gilbert snatched a cookie and handed it to her. "The doctors want to do some more tests, but you should be able to leave tomorrow. They don't want you to fly until all the results are in, which won't be until after the holidays. We'd love for you to spend Christmas with us."

"Si'il te plaît?" chimed Luca.

"I'd love to, but Marti will be so disappointed."

Gilbert patted his forehead. "I forgot. She kept calling your mobile. I hope you do not mind, but I answered her call and told her. She is very worried." He reached into his pocket. "She said to call her no matter the time." He gave Claire her phone.

"Merci. I appreciate your answering Marti's call."

Gilbert clapped his hands. "Let us give Claire some privacy. We will return tomorrow morning. Do you wish for me to retrieve your luggage from the hotel? I know the owner, and she will personally pack your things."

Claire's arms and legs felt like they weighed more than Santa's sack of toys. "Yes. Please thank Madame Justine for me. Oh, and don't peek at the wrapped gift."

Gilbert smiled, bent down, and kissed her cheek. "À demain."

She wanted to kiss him back.

Luca placed the box of cookies on her lap and kissed both her cheeks. "You make us very happy, Madame Claire."

Tears threatened. "Me too."

"We say, 'Moi aussi.'"

Luca's earnestness warmed her. "Moi aussi. À demain."

Luca nodded. "You are a very fast learner."

Waving, they departed.

How on earth had she jumped into a river, much less saved Luca? She couldn't swim, could she?

Chapter 24

Claire dialed Marti.

"Jeel-Bear told me," her voice boomed. "I've been worried sick. I was about to book a flight to come and get you. How are you feeling?"

Claire held the phone away from her ear. "Oh, Marti, I love you. I'm so sorry you were worried. I'm okay."

"No, 'okay' is not the answer I am looking for. You jumped into an ice-cold river and saved your husband's son! I'm not only worried about your physical health, but also your mental stability."

"You don't have to—"

"Yes, I do. Are you nuts? Weren't there other people who could have gone in after him?"

"I knew Luca was going in after that dog before he did. He's a little boy, a good-hearted little boy who loves animals, and he wanted to save that dog."

"Where was Gilbert? I wanted to ask him, but I didn't want to be rude."

"He needed to use the restroom after the boat trip."

"Boat trip? You hate boats! You hate the water!"

"I wanted to spend time with Luca, and he wanted to take a boat ride."

"Eeeeeeeeeeeek! I'm tearing my hair out."

"Take deep breaths. Come on, do it with me. Inhale…"

Marti's laughter boomed. "You sound like a shrink."

Claire laughed with her. Her laughter released the pressure and tension in her chest, and it felt so good. "Do your teenager patients give you this much grief?"

"No. And that's saying a lot."

"I'm so sorry. But please help me."

"Gilbert sounds like he's very concerned about you and very helpful. Is he as handsome as he sounds?"

"More than you think."

Marti crowed. "Don't sit facing the sun. Sit with your back to the sun when you're across from Gilbert."

"Huh? Why?"

"Sunlight shows your wrinkles."

Claire laughed. "He saw me looking like a drowned rat. I don't think it will matter."

"Just sayin'."

White freesia and red roses surrounded by pine boughs and silver pinecones, sitting in a white vase next to her bed, caught Claire's eye. Had Gilbert brought them?

"You asked me to help you. What do you need me to help you with?"

Claire let out a long exhale and tilted her head to her right shoulder, then her left. "Marti, I don't think I can swim."

"Are you CRAZY?" Marti's voice was like a buffeting wind. "You could've drowned!"

"Listen, I don't know why I jumped in after Luca. I just—"

"Claire!" Her voice softened like butter. "You risked your life for him, just like any loving mother would."

Claire pushed an exhale. "I've been wracking my mind trying to remember...what it is I want to remember, I don't know...but I've got to remember because whatever is hiding in this dark place in me is what scared me from becoming a mother."

"Oh boy, we're in over our heads here. I know a psychiatrist, but she won't work with you until she's met you."

"I don't want a psychiatrist." Claire tapped the speaker icon and placed the phone on her lap. "When I try to remember what happened, it's like I'm in a dark tunnel and there is no light anywhere. I hear rushing water, and I'm cold, and I smell mud, but I keep walking."

"Do it now and tell me what you feel."

Claire rubbed her eyes. An ache weighed heavily in her heart.

"See Luca as you did by the river," urged Marti.

"As he took a running start, I saw a life ring hanging on the wall, just beyond. After Luca jumped, I grabbed it." Something squeezed her heart so hard, she gasped. "Oh my God, I didn't want what happened to me to happen to Luca!" she cried.

"What happened to you, Claire? Can you see yourself?"

"The river..." Brightness glowed. Her vision grew fuzzy, like mist rolling through the room. "I don't know. Everything's gone dark again."

"Luca might have drowned if you hadn't jumped in after him," Marti whispered.

Claire squeezed and opened her eyes. Her sweater hung from a hook on the wall. A jagged rip running down the sleeve proved Gilbert was right. The dog must have torn her sleeve as he dragged her to the surface.

"This means that you must have almost drowned. Do you remember anything like that?"

"What? No. My mother never took me to a beach."

"That you remember." Marti countered.

"Is that what's hidden in the darkness?"

"Sometimes not remembering is the body's method of self-preservation."

"You mean the dark is protecting me the way David protected me by not telling me about Luca?"

"Possibly."

"I want to know the truth."

"Do you feel safe with Gilbert?"

Claire inhaled the scent of freesia and pine. "Yes."

"Ask if he will help you. You shouldn't be alone when you do remember."

"Oh, great." She fell back into the pillow.

"Do you recall what you said when I asked you why you were afraid of having kids?"

"That I'd be a bad mother."

"Might that be because you *had* a bad mother?"

"She wasn't bad, just cold."

"Not if she nearly let you drown. She was neglectful. Remember your last Christmas with her, when she neglected to have food in the house? I hope you understand that by risking your own life, you did exactly what every good mother would have done for her own child."

"I did?"

"You would have made a wonderful mother, Claire. But you need to learn how to swim. Gilbert said he performed CPR on you until the paramedics arrived. You weren't breathing on your own."

"He...didn't tell me." She rubbed her breastbone. "That's why my chest hurts."

"He cares deeply for you. I think the poor man was in tears when he told me, but I don't know for sure because I was already crying, myself."

"I care about them too." She had cared about Luca since her first glimpse of his photo, and she'd cared about Gilbert the morning he'd taken her to the patisserie. She inhaled calming breaths. But she didn't know whether she should let them know she cared. She didn't know how to...behave. Did she trust them? Did she love them? Yes. She loved and trusted them. Both of them. Gilbert a little differently, but, underneath the obvious attraction, she loved him. She didn't want to leave them. She couldn't leave Luca. How did David leave his son?

Her mind whirled. David had been a loving, caring, generous husband, but she wanted more than love and security. She craved...closeness. She had missed that opportunity with David—she'd built a wall between them that distanced them, probably because she hadn't been close to knowing all of herself.

She wanted to truly know Luca and Gilbert. She knew some of Luca and Gilbert's losses, their grief, and their happiness. She wanted to share all of it—disappointments, successes, failures, triumphs—everything.

She didn't want to be protected from the dark ugliness that lurked inside of her, like a mythological Kraken. She wanted to expose the giant octopus and release herself from its terrible tentacles. That Kraken was a part of her, but it wasn't who she was. She was a loving and kind person, who was also frightened.

"Claire?" Marti's voice brought her back to the hospital room. "I said, do you see the irony that you spent most of your career designing a swimsuit with a built-in life-preserver?"

"What?" Claire sat straight up. "I think I started that when I was at boarding school. While other girls were stuffing their bras with socks, I was stuffing bikini tops with inflated balloons and blocks of Styrofoam. Why did the irony never occur to me? Why was I so obsessed?"

"You wanted to save people, like you saved Luca...and like someone saved you when you were a child." Marti hummed a lullaby, a bit of which Claire recognized, something having to do with pretty horses.

Claire rested back against the pillows, entranced by comfort, but she straightened. How had she known that lullaby? *All the pretty little horses.* Had a nun sung it to her? She pressed her fingers to her temples, but the image didn't arrive. "I love you, Marti. I need to think through a lot of stuff. Especially why David never told me about Luca, but I'm so tired. Okay if I call you tomorrow?"

"Of course. Call anytime and often, otherwise, I'm booking a flight, and they're not cheap!"

Love flooded Claire as she said goodbye and put her phone away.

Darkness yawned before her. She searched for a thread that would lead her to a long-buried memory. The muddy scent of the Ill River had caused her to shiver, and the sound of rushing water had made her feel clammy. Whatever she wasn't remembering happened at a river.

She had to build up her courage to ask Gilbert for his help. She knew whatever she was hiding was going to be painful when she finally dragged it into the light. Fighting the Kraken in her was going to be a terrible battle.

She ate one of Sister Georgette's cookies. Ate another. And another. She wished she'd bought another box.

CHAPTER 25

Jingle Bell Rock blared over the car speakers as Gilbert drove south on the Wine Route. Luca, singing at the top of his lungs, hugged Remy in the backseat. Claire sat in the front, Remy's hot panting warming the back of her neck. She owed her life to Remy's cousin, who'd ripped her sweater, and, in honor of him, she'd be buying Remy bones for the rest of his dear life.

She planned on being a good guest, wouldn't cause any trouble at all, wouldn't disrupt their routine. They wouldn't even know she was there with them. She'd pick up after herself, help with the cooking and the dishes and laundry, and play ball with Remy. And she wouldn't stay a day longer than she had to. David would want her to stay with them, wouldn't he?

They arrived at the château, and, on shaky legs, she accepted Gilbert's hand as he helped her out of the car.

Luca raced ahead, opened the hand-carved wooden door sporting a wreath trimmed in silver beads and an owl ornament, and held out his hands. "Close your eyes, Madame Claire. We have a surprise for you."

Squeezing her eyes shut, she held Luca's hands and allowed him to lead her. He stopped. "D'accord. Regarde!"

A Christmas tree, decorated with white lights and bird, dog, cow, fish, monkey, giraffe, peacock, piglets, and elephant ornaments soared in the corner, reminding her of the ornaments she and her friends made at the convent. Her poodle ornament would have fit right in. The cozy living room was tastefully furnished with antique pine tables, a leather couch, and green velvet covered chairs. Gilbert crouched down and lit a fire in a fireplace that was the size of her master bathroom in Seattle.

"What a beautiful grand room and huge tree!" she exclaimed.

"Le grand sapin." Luca's face glowed.

She repeated the phrase. "It must be fifteen feet high."

"Five meters. Very close guess." Gilbert grinned.

"Onc and I cut the tree down in the forest up in the mountains and dragged it to the car."

"How did you get the ornaments on those high branches and the angel on top?" she asked.

"We put the angel on first and then put up the tree. I sat on Onc's shoulders and used a long pole to hang ornaments at the top."

"Glass of wine?" Gilbert asked. He took a corkscrew off the bar and began opening a bottle of red. His muscular arms made quick work of the task. Marti would agree, he was too, too handsome.

"That would be heavenly." She sat on the comfy, worn sofa before an antique hand-carved pine coffee table. She was as comfortable here as she was at home, more so, since she'd been lonely at home.

Luca took what Claire thought was a cookie from a jar on a side table. Remy knew better and plopped down before Luca who held his hand out to the dog. "Donne la patte, Remy."

The dog pawed Luca's open palm, and Luca gave him the treat. Luca gave her a bone. "Now your turn."

"Remy, come." The dog trotted over, sat in front of her, and rested his slobbering chin on her lap, his huge brown eyes begging for sustenance. Claire laughed. "Donne... hmmm...donne la..." she shook her head. That phrase was too cumbersome. Remy would have to become bilingual. She held out the treat. "Shake." The dog gave her his paw, she shook it and bestowed his prize. She was not only falling in love with Luca, but she was beginning to genuinely like his dog.

Gilbert placed a glass of wine on the table before her. "Would you please turn on the lamp next to you?"

She reached and pulled a chain. Warm light drenched the room and lit up silver-framed photos along the table. One of Luca as an infant, another of Gilbert and Luca wearing matching berets, and another: David and Sophie, holding a grinning Luca between them.

Nausea waved through her. David and Sophie should be here, sharing this joy with their son. But here she was, celebrating Christmas, only to leave them, just like David did. They still missed David, and she'd be doing the same thing by leaving them in a week.

A crackling noise startled her. Gilbert added kindling to the fire, the muscles of his back straining against his shirt as he grabbed a log and set it on the grate.

Where was her loyalty to David, thinking Gilbert handsome, feeling attracted to him? How could she consider falling in love with Gilbert if she still loved David? But she wanted more in a relationship than she'd had with David. Good grief. She should have stayed with Sister Georgette at the convent.

Gilbert slapped wood dust from his hands. "Time for bed, Luca."

"But Onc, you haven't made dinner."

"You had a hamburger. Are you still hungry?"

"Dinner for Madame Claire."

"I'm not hungry, and I'm so exhausted. I would like to rest." Claire stood, upsetting the glass, spilling red wine across the coffee table. "Oh, I am so very sorry." She looked about and, finding nothing to wipe up the spill before it dripped onto the antique carpet, she ripped off her scarf and mopped up the wine.

Gilbert's hand stopped hers. "It's all right Claire. Salt will absorb the stain. Do not worry." He dumped a salt-cellar onto the wine dripping onto the carpet, making the spill look like a mound of pink snow. "We keep these dishes of salt on nearly every table all around the house, which is more than two-hundred and fifty years old and has seen just as many spills, if not more, just like that carpet."

Her heartbeat galloped. She had to leave, get out, now. She picked up the soaked scarf and held her hand to catch the drips. "I'll clean the rug in the morning." She turned and headed for the stairs. "My room is where?"

Gilbert was next to her in an instant. He took the scarf. "The last door on the right. First, I will put this to soak.

Then, I'll bring your bag up in a minute." He moved to touch her hand, but she backed away, ran to the stairs, and started to climb.

"Good night, Luca." She raced up the stairs to the end of the hall and shut the door behind her.

CHAPTER 26

She locked the door, leaned against it, and sighed. A sense of tranquility fell over her. The room was out of a decorating magazine, furnished in antique white pine and French linen drapes and bed hangings. She hoped the framed Monets on the wall were prints. Gilbert had done all this. His choice of plaid and complementing print fabrics was brave and elegant. Marti would be impressed. A lovely prison she'd sentenced herself to.

She had promised Marti and herself she'd have the courage to ask Gilbert to help her. But she'd used every drop of courage she possessed to remain calm after looking at that photograph of Sophie, Luca, and David—the happy family that she didn't belong to. It was too early in Seattle to call Marti, even if she'd told her to call anytime, this was not an emergency. Claire could handle these emotions herself...maybe.

Her face burned as she searched to identify what she was feeling—like a sense of having been slapped. She was jealous. Jealous of something she'd known nothing about for at least seven years of her marriage. Beneath her jealousy lay a swamp of betrayal.

She paced. Why wasn't she seeing David for who he was? He'd kept Luca a secret. For years. David might have been afraid to tell her about Luca, but she struggled to comprehend how he'd left his son after every visit. She'd been with the child for a few hours over the past two days and already missed him. She'd never figure out how David could leave Luca.

She'd been loyal to her husband her entire married life, but David wasn't here anymore. He'd betrayed her by keeping Luca a secret. She wasn't betraying David by feeling attracted to Gilbert. She rubbed her thighs and saw the wine had stained her caramel pants. She groaned and looked around the room for a saltcellar and found one on the desk. Folding the slacks into the bathroom sink, she sprinkled the salt over the stain and turned on the cold water.

A knock startled her. That was Gilbert, and she was half naked. She grabbed a chenille throw from the bed and wrapped it around her hips like a skirt. "Come in."

The doorknob clicked. "It's locked."

"Oh, how did that happen?" Could she pretend she couldn't unlock it? She gnawed at her chapped lip. Stop lying. Clutching her blanket-skirt, she bent and unlocked the door with a flick of her finger.

He placed her roller bag on the floor, encircled her in his arms, and pulled her to him.

She put up her hands and resisted for half a second, then leaned into him, inhaling the cedar scent of his cologne.

"I am sorry about the photograph. I should have put it away, but I forgot. It must have been a shock for you."

How had he known in an instant how she felt? She nodded. He rubbed her back. His heart beat against her palms, strong, slow, steady.

"David and Sophie admired and respected one another, but they were only friends."

And David had kept Sophie a secret, as well as Gilbert and Luca. A stiffness spread across her shoulders. She was angry with David. Marti would say: About time.

"Would you like to return to the salon? The fire is lonely, and so am I."

She reluctantly backed away. Her blanket-skirt fell to her ankles.

"There's a fluffy robe hanging in the armoire." He grinned.

She was surprised she wasn't embarrassed. She wanted him to look at her. Being in his arms felt safe, and she already missed his warmth. "D'accord. I'll be down in a minute."

"Your French lessons are going well." He quietly closed the door behind him.

She began unpacking her bag and held David's photo. *I feel cheated that you never shared Luca with me. It feels good to be angry with you.* Guilt swept in and back out. David always protected her, but whatever he protected her from was cloaked in darkness. Why hadn't he helped her to uncover her feelings? Or encourage her to excavate them herself? Or at least urge her to talk to her best friend, who happened to be a doctor. She placed the photo in a drawer, under her clothes. David wasn't alive anymore. She needed to see him for who he really was, not who she thought he'd been.

The darkness in her life had restricted her and her marriage from growing. She wanted an intimate relationship, and she'd have one if it killed her. Hiding from the octopus's tentacles was no longer possible. She aimed to shine light on that Kraken and evict him from her life.

She freshened her makeup, changed into her nightgown, put on the fluffy white robe embroidered with tiny pink rosebuds, and fussed with her hair.

Gilbert was right, David wouldn't want her to be lonely. He'd want her to be happy. And since she had the rest of her life to live, she wanted to be happy, too.

CHAPTER 27

A platter of cold roast chicken, baguette slices, olives, cornichons, grapes, and three cheeses sat in the center of the coffee table. How did the French put together elegant, gourmet meals in a few minutes? It would take at least an hour for her to drive to the grocery store and buy a rotisserie chicken and potato chips.

Two wine glasses, plates and napkins rested on the coffee table. She sat on the couch and tucked her feet up under the robe.

Gilbert carried logs and placed them on the fire. "Would you prefer red or white wine?"

"Does white stain less?"

"Salt works on both."

"David would advise that the white goes best with the chicken?" she asked.

He dusted off his hands. "Probably. It was his favorite."

"I'm angry with David. I'll take the red."

He poured the wine, handed her a glass, and clinked his glass to hers. "Welcome." Golden specs in his blue-gray eyes glittered in the soft light.

"Merci." She sipped.

"Your friend Marti told me you cannot swim."

"I don't think I can. But I know water safety."

"Then why did you risk your life?" His voice was a whisper.

"I didn't want Luca to experience what happened to me." She tightened the belt of the robe.

"You almost drowned?"

"I think I may have. I can't remember. Marti told me I won't be free of this fear until I remember what caused it."

He sat next to her and rested his arm on the back of the couch. "I noticed you seemed a bit anxious before we boarded the boat and when it embarked. And then again, when we walked along the river."

"I was. I felt like I was in a place from long ago. Darkness dropped over me, and I was petrified with fright."

"What do you remember about the past?"

She gulped some wine. "A muddy scent. The roaring of rushing water." She closed her eyes. "I don't think I can do this."

"I'm here for you. You're safe." Gilbert took her wine glass from her. "What else do you recall?"

"Everything is cold and dark."

He put his arm around her and pulled her to him. "I'm here."

His gentle voice broke open a barrier she was too weary to hold. The sensation of water sluiced over her, drenched her, swamped her.

Pressure built around her, and the desire to let go pulled at her. She moaned, pitched forward, covered her head with her arms, and abandoned herself to the darkness.

"Tell me what's happening." Gilbert's voice was far away.

She pulled her legs out from under her and tried to stand, struggling against his strong arms. As if caught in a whirlpool, water and debris and mud swirled around her, sucking her away from him.

She hunched over watching that day play in her mind. "I'm at a park, with trees and picnic tables, and a beach on the side of a river. I'm playing tag with a little girl, about my age, in the river. We're laughing and splashing each other."

Her heartbeat quickened, and her arms stiffened. "My foot slips on a slimy rock, and I fall. The water pulls my head under and tears me away from the little girl into deeper water. I'm kicking and flailing my arms, but the water won't let me go, and it drags me against the rocky river bottom. It's getting darker, and I don't have any more air. I push my legs down, and kick with all my might, but my feet don't reach the bottom. The water speeds up, whirling me around, scraping me against a fallen tree, its branches claw me. I clutch at the leaves, but they slide through my fingers, I'm trying to pull myself away, but the current slams me against a rock." Her head snapped back like it must have when she hit the rock.

She wrapped her hands around her head. "Everything is black...and silent."

Gilbert brought her firmly against him and pulled her back onto the couch. "What happened then? It's okay, I won't let anything hurt you. Take a deep breath."

She inhaled and tried to focus through the ocean of darkness. The image of the park brightened, and she watched her child-self like she was watching a movie. "People were standing on the shore, shouting. A dark haired and bearded man carried me from the river onto the sand and wrapped his arm around my waist and was pounding my back. I vomited buckets of muddy water. I was choking and crying. My head throbbed. Blood was running down my arms and legs. "The man wrapped me in a towel and picked me up, shouting at my mother."

"Where is your mother?"

"Standing under a willow tree, holding a book." Claire's voice sounded strangely calm and far away. "Mother walked toward him. He yelled at her, calling her—it must have been the word negligent—because I didn't know what it meant, and I thought he said, negligee, and I remember thinking my mother would never wear such a thing. He said something about the hospital, and she crossed her arms and said, 'No.'"

Gilbert held her tighter.

She squirmed to turn and look at him. "How could she *not* take me to the hospital? I nearly drowned."

Gilbert's eyes flooded with the alarm and concern she thought her mother should have felt.

Claire got up and paced with fury, causing another memory to break through the fog like water bursting through a dam. "The man carried me to his car and laid me on the backseat, with my head in his daughter's lap. She was the little girl I'd been playing tag with, and she held my hand, all the time telling me I would be okay, and patting my cuts with a wet towel."

Claire stood still, silent, letting the heavy pain of truth settle in her. "That child was more nurturing to me than my own mother."

She began pacing again, shaking her hands and flinging a pulsing rage from her fingers. "So many doctors and nurses tended to me, asking question after question about my mother, who wasn't there. Why wasn't she there?"

She fell into an overstuffed chair, bent over, and rested her head in her hands. Her anger dwindled. "My mother left me there for three days."

Gilbert knelt before her and swept her hair from her eyes.

"These memories keep coming. I can't stop them." A moan seeped out. "I was glad for the good food and the warmth of the nurses and doctors. I remember looking for the dark-haired man in the hospital, wondering where he and his little girl were. I wanted to thank them, but they never came.

The nurses played memory games and cards with me, got me to sing songs with them..." She tapped her forehead. That's where she knew the *Pretty Little Horses* song. "They made jokes and used sock puppets with funny names to remove my bandages. Without the nurses, I'd have been all alone." She gulped for air. "For the first time in my seven years of living, I was having fun."

"You were about Luca's age." Gilbert caressed her cheek.

She nodded. "I can't imagine not loving a little seven-year-old girl." Her heart ached as another memory crested. "Then my mother and a woman dressed in a stiff suit, like the ones my mother wore, carrying a purse stuffed with papers and wearing shoes that were the shape and color of bricks, arrived. I wondered if she was in the Army—she had a mustache. The Army woman told my mother to dress me. My mother held out my clothes to a nurse, and the nurse helped me into my church dress, sweater, and shoes."

Claire thought it was sorrow creasing Gilbert's cheeks and dulling his eyes. She was sorry her story was causing him pain, and she was grateful to him for being with her.

She wiped sweat and tears from her face, stood on shaky legs, walked to the couch, and collapsed onto it. "Without a word or smile, the two of them drove me to a convent in Vermont. What a fun pair they were; neither of them spoke during the whole trip, and it took five hours."

Gilbert sat next to her.

Claire pounded her fists into the couch cushions. "And my mother left me there. The nuns explained my mother was too ill to care for me, and she was going to a hospital. I thought the Army woman was helping my sick mother, but now I comprehend she was there to ensure my mother didn't take me swimming again."

A sob convulsed her. She curled into a tiny ball, as if hiding from the monster who was no Kraken, but her mother. "She never loved me," Claire's voice was distant, like it wasn't coming from her. "All my life, I thought I was unlovable, unworthy of love. But children are worthy of love just by being born. It's taken me fifty years to rec- ognize that it didn't matter who her child was, my mother was incapable of loving anyone."

Gilbert gave her his handkerchief and kissed the top of her head.

A strange laugh seized her. "I was grateful to my mother for taking me to the convent, but now I realize she didn't do it out of kindness, she was forced to. The woman who I thought was from the army was probably from Child Protective Services. The nuns saved my life. They loved me and cared for me and nurtured me." Sobs ebbed and flowed until Claire lay on her side, panting on the couch. Gilbert gathered her into his arms and sat with her nestled against him.

She pressed her head to his chest, the sound of his strong, steady heartbeat comforting her, making her feel safe. She wiped and opened her eyes to the sparkling lights of the Christmas tree, glistening roast chicken, and ruby red wine. "I need a drink."

Gilbert's laugh rumbled.

"I'm ravenous, too."

He sat her up and handed her the glass of wine.

She sniffed and sipped. "A hint of nutmeg?" She drank. "Definitely nutmeg."

His eyebrows arched. "Maybe one in a thousand people notice that. I can't taste or smell it, but Sophie could."

"And David?"

He shook his head.

Claire took a long drink and set the glass down. "Now I think I know what David was protecting me from. He must have at least suspected my mother didn't love me and didn't want to force me to acknowledge such a painful truth." She brought her shoulders up and let them drop.

"My mother hated me." She took another drink. "She was sick and inhuman."

She rubbed her hands along the embroidered flowers of the robe. "I was terrified to be a mother, because I guess subconsciously, I thought I'd be a monster, just like her. And I've lived enshrouded by this darkness that has prevented me from fully living."

"Even people who know how to swim can get caught in strong currents and drown. You may know how to swim. Nevertheless, you risked your life to save Luca. Every loving mother would have done that, Claire. Never fear becoming anything like your mother." He spread some cheese on a baguette slice and offered it.

She bit and closed her eyes. "Mmmm. Nuttiness...and pear?"

"No taste will ever escape your palate."

"At least my tastebuds have been living a full life."

He offered her a drumstick. "Now that you are in France, you'll discover they've only just begun to live."

She kissed his cheek. "Merci. For being with me. For helping me through the dark."

"I am happy to be with you. I love being with you." He curled his arm around her.

"I am happy to be with you, and Luca, too." She held out her glass, and he refilled it. "Do you know why David didn't tell me about Luca?"

He ran his fingers through his hair. "He told us he would one day, and when he didn't show up, Sophie and I feared he told you and you would not allow him to return. But that wasn't true. Did he not tell you in his letter?"

"What letter?"

"He told us he had included a copy of a letter for you, should anything happen to him, with his will."

"David didn't leave a will—at least not one I or our attorney have found."

"His letter, and perhaps his will, is in the envelope I brought to you—it must be in your bag, because you gave the envelope to Madame Justine, and she assured me she packed everything."

What a jigsaw puzzle David had left for her. Had she not been fired and not needed David's comfort, she'd still not know of Luca or Gilbert. Had she given away his clothing without checking his pockets, she might never have known. "I'll save reading his letter for tomorrow. I'd like to enjoy being here with you now."

Gilbert took a sip of wine. "Do you know why I never married?"

"You never met the right woman?"

He rubbed his jaw. "I thought I had...twice, but they both accused me of the same thing. They thought I was afraid of commitment."

"You? You are totally devoted to Luca and the winery."

He tipped his head and his eyebrows rose. "Do you want to know the real reason?"

"Of course."

"I was terrified of having children."

She pressed her hand to her throat. "But you're a wonderful father to Luca."

He shifted his jaw side to side. "Sophie and I were the luckiest children in the world, because we had terrific parents. Unfortunately, they both died very young. Although I was in my twenties, I still needed parenting. My papa was such a great man, I feared I'd never measure up to him, and I was afraid to try, so I never married. But when I saw Luca for the very first time, it was a coup de foudre."

"Love hit you like a lightning bolt." David had ensured she knew that phrase, for he had experienced it at his first sight of her.

"It did. Even though Luca was all red and wrinkled, screaming, battling the air with his chestnut-sized fists, my heart burst with love for him. At that moment I promised him I'd love him forever and never let any harm come to him." He ran his finger along Claire's cheek. "Another reason I am so very grateful to you."

"We're quite a pair, madly in love with the thing we most feared."

Laughter burst like Champagne bubbles. Claire laughed so hard she fell onto her side and rolled over onto her back. Her laughter shook the tightness from her chest and the pain from her heart.

Gilbert caressed her cheek, and she wished she'd spent more time on her makeup. He leaned over her and smoothed a curl behind her ear. Warmth and excitement tingled in her.

She placed her palm over the center of his chest, looking deeply into his eyes.

His lips gently pressed hers, and she lost herself in kissing him.

He wrapped his arms around her, and she allowed herself to be buoyed by him. She could float like this forever.

CHAPTER 28

Bright sunshine filled the salon and woke Claire. Swimming out from under three duvets, she pulled herself to sit up on the sofa. On the coffee table sat a French press pot of coffee, a jug of warm milk, plate of croissants, jar of jam, and a note from Gilbert explaining he and Luca went shopping and hoped she would enjoy her breakfast.

Claire took her coffee and croissants to her room, found the large envelope in her suitcase, and sat on the bed. She pressed David's last letter to her heart, remembering his love, knowing she now had the courage to know whatever had made him keep Luca a secret.

My dearest Claire,

I apologize for not telling you about Luca. I will try to explain.

Throughout our marriage, I begged you to start a family with me. I deeply regret not pushing you to understand why you feared being a mother, but the one time I did, you left for two days, and I didn't want to risk you doing that again. On our fifteenth anniversary, when you claimed you wanted children but weren't ready, I realized you never would be ready. After that conversation I tried with all my heart to give up my desire to have a child, because I loved you and our marriage, and I knew if I pushed you, our marriage would be altered and might have ended.

I couldn't imagine my life without you, so I struggled to let go of my dream. Soon after that I met Sophie who desired a child. I thought that because you never wanted to accompany me to France, you'd never know if I enabled Sophie to live her dream. I would never cheat on you, and so I donated sperm to Sophie through a clinic in Colmar.

I should have discussed my donation to Sophie with you, but I could not have borne it if you had told me not to do it.

I never imagined that I could love anyone as much as I love you. But the first glimpse of Luca was a coup de foudre. I love him with all my heart, as I do you. And I cannot imagine losing either of you.

After I met him, I should have told you about Luca, but I could not have borne it if you forced me to choose between you or if you stopped loving me.

My choice allowed me to continue loving you and loving my child.

Words cannot adequately convey my apology for hurting you, Claire. But I do ask for forgiveness.

When I weighed the risks of telling you about Luca, terror shook me. Oddly, at that moment my compassion for you grew. I tried so many times to talk to you about your apprehension that I believe stemmed from your mother and imprisoned your life. And it wasn't until the thought of losing you and Luca struck me with horror that I understood the depth of your trepidation.

I hope you will one day have the courage to confront and unentangle yourself from that fright. I wish I could have helped you slay that dragon.

But who am I to talk? I don't have the courage to write a will, for doing so would reveal my son. Being a coward, I left discovering Luca in your hands. That is why I always carried his photo in my favorite jacket, in the hope that should something happen to me, you would seek him out on your own—if you wanted to.

I am sorry I hurt and betrayed you.

But I'm not sorry I have helped bring a vibrant, intelligent, and beautiful boy into this world. I hope his love warms your life as it has warmed mine. I hope you have fallen in love with Luca. I hope you will learn what a wonderful mother you could have been.

I hope in time you can forgive me and accept Luca as my last gift to you.

Your adoring husband,
David

She wiped tears, refolded the letter, and stuffed it in the envelope.

"You left discovering Luca in my hands?" Anger pulsed up her arms, and she threw the letter across the room. "Well, you could have left a few more clues."

Marti's words rang in her mind, *David was always protective of you. I am sure he didn't tell you because he didn't want to hurt you.*

"Wrong! He protected himself. Even he admits he was a coward." She grabbed her phone and stabbed Marti's number. The call went to voicemail. "Call me. I've solved the mystery of why my husband didn't leave a will."

She ended the call and tossed her phone on the bed. She didn't need Marti to help her figure out how she felt. She was angry, rightfully so. It was good David was dead because if he wasn't she'd murder him.

She dug out the photo of David she'd placed in a drawer and shoved it in her empty suitcase.

Scenes from her marriage whirled around in her mind, dizzying her. She flopped onto the bed and watched her interactions with David in a brighter light with darker shadows. Marti would say processing this would take a while. She rolled up her sleeves. She was ready to dig in.

But first, she was going to celebrate Christmas with a child she loved...and a man she was falling in love with.

CHAPTER 29

A jazzy Christmas carol played on the radio in the château kitchen, which was larger than the salon. Even Sister Georgette's kitchen was a quarter of the size of this. A stove with eight, double-ringed burners shone in the bright morning light. A table for twenty sat near the wall of windows overlooking the vineyard.

Sister Georgette had allowed Claire to photograph her cookie recipe, so all Claire had to do was find the ingredients. Unable to find a mixer, she was up to her elbows in batter when Remy loped through the door toward her. This time she sat on the floor before he could knock her over and let him lick her hands and wooden spoon.

Gilbert walked into the kitchen and shouted, "Remy!" The dog bit the spoon, pulled it from her hand, and scampered to his bed in the corner, where his tongue chased every morsel of dough.

Claire laughed. "It's all right. I'm getting used to him."

Luca arrived carrying a bundle of packages. "Remy!" The child fell to the floor in giggles.

Gilbert helped Claire to her feet and handed her a bar of soap.

Still laughing, she washed up. "I'll bet he got at least three cookies off my hands and that spoon."

Luca ran to her. "Was there any chocolate in it? Chocolate very bad for dogs."

His concern for Remy rippled across her heart. "No, no chocolate. Only dried fruit and nuts, eggs, flour, oh, and brandy."

Luca ran over and rubbed the dog's belly. "Ah, he gets wine every time it spills. He should be okay, but we watch him." He ran over to his packages. "Madame Claire, I have an early Christmas gift for you." He checked with Gilbert. "Is it okay to give it to her now, Onc?"

Gilbert smiled. "Bien sûr."

Luca pulled out a chair at the long wooden table and patted it. "Please sit down. No French lessons today. I give you the day off."

Drying her hands, she sat. Luca placed a red envelope before her.

She shook it. "Is it a diamond necklace?"

Luca rolled his eyes.

She sniffed it. "A puppy?"

"And make Remy jealous? Non."

She held the envelope up to the light. "A widescreen TV."

"That is so American."

"Sorry. Okay, I'll open it if you're not going to give me any clues." She ripped the flap up and pulled out a certificate: a week's membership to the Colmar Community Pool. She gulped.

Luca tucked his head up under her arm. "You are too old not to know how to swim Madame Claire. I will teach you."

A laugh burst from her belly. Luca smiled his dimpled smile. Loving Luca was a coup de foudre.

Gilbert rested his hands on his hips, shaking his head at his incorrigible son.

Claire laughed so hard, Luca grabbed her arm to keep her on her chair. She wiped at happy tears. "Merci, Luca. It's just what I wanted."

Gilbert grew concerned. "I should have asked, do you have a bathing suit?"

Still laughing, Claire said, "I can design—" She pressed her lips together. Nope, she was done with that obsession. "I can buy one."

Luca jumped up. "First lesson next week! We practice breathing before we go to the pool."

"I think Claire would like to finish making the cookies first," Gilbert said in a soothing voice.

"D'accord. I must wrap gifts." He lugged the bags after him into the salon.

"I'm sorry. It was his idea, and I could not talk him out of it." Gilbert sat next to her.

"He's right. I am too old not to know how to swim." She stuffed the certificate back in the envelope. "Thank you for telling me about the letter. David didn't tell me about Luca because he feared I might force him to choose between us, and he could not bear life without Luca or me."

He nodded. "I can understand, but he missed out on knowing you deeply."

"And I him." Claire shrugged at the loss she could do nothing about. She had to forgive herself and David.

"Some of the test results arrived." Gilbert held both her hands. "You have saved Luca's life, twice." His eyes reddened.

A sinking sensation plunged through her. "He has Sitosterolemia."

Gilbert stared at their hands. "They think he may. My father died of a heart attack when he was younger than David. Luca could have inherited the condition from either parent or from both Sophie *and* David. The doctor wants to conduct more tests, but he prescribed medicine that Luca must take every day, and he must follow a special diet. If he does these things, there is no reason why he cannot live a long life." Tears sat in his eyes.

Claire clamped her hand over a sob. Tears of relief sprang. "Marti wanted me to wait until after the holidays to find Luca, but I was terrified something could happen to him at any time. David must have sent me to save his son."

Gilbert smiled. "Maybe so, but he certainly didn't expect you to save him twice. You're a—Americans say, 'rockstar?'"

Claire picked up a spatula and, pretending it was a microphone, mouthed the words to *Santa Claus is Coming to Town*.

Gilbert laughed and took away the spoon. "I have a question for you."

She loved the warmth cascading through her.

His eyes searched hers. "Would you like to work here at the winery and stay with Luca and me?"

"For Christmas?"

"For Christmas, and the new year, and—beyond."

Joy bubbled up in her, and she floated on its buoyancy until she remembered Seattle. She put her hand over his. "What would I do for a job?"

"I am a good vigneron, but Sophie was the vintner. I don't know if my wines will be as good as those Sophie created. But, with your palate I believe we would come very close to those award-winning vintages. The winery needs your palate. And Luca and I need you."

"Wouldn't I have to go through a lot of red tape? Get a Visa..."

"It would be a simple process since you'd already have a job offer."

"What does Luca want?"

"It was his idea." Gilbert's smile was broad. "His and Remy's."

She smiled and searched his blue-gray eyes, surrounded by lines wrought by years of laughter and worry and sorrow and joy.

"And if the wine doesn't work out, we can redesign this place together." His eyes were sincere, kind, trusting.

She was falling in love with him, and she didn't want to live five thousand miles away. "Thank you. You are very thoughtful. It is a wonderful offer and opportunity. I'll need to think about it. But I can assure you, that's all I'll be thinking about."

She wrapped her arms around his neck and kissed his cheek.

CHAPTER 30

Snowflakes swirled outside the French doors and draped the vineyard in a sparkling white duvet. The twinkling white lights of the Christmas tree bathed the great room in a soft glow. The Yule log snapped, and through the speakers a children's choir sang *Il est né le divin enfant*.

Puppies of different breeds were printed all over Luca's pajamas. He snuggled next to Claire, his arm around Remy, who snoozed on the couch beside him.

Claire had expected Luca to be uncontrollably excited on Christmas morning, but she sensed his heart was heavy, missing his parents. Gilbert, too, was quiet. She missed David and, although she'd never met Sophie, Claire missed her, too. At that moment she was surprised she had forgotten that her and David's anniversary had been the day before, and she'd not acknowledged it. She thought it odd that as she was getting to know more about David, his presence seemed to dim. Was that because she was getting to know Luca? Or was she letting David go?

They sipped their café au lait, watched the snow, listened to the music.

"Are they singing about baby Jesus being born?" she asked Luca.

He nodded. "It was Maman's favorite carol."

Claire pressed him to her, hoping he felt safe, cared for, loved. Oddly, she felt those same emotions just by holding him close. She'd not known what she was missing as a child, and she pitied her mother who never had this experience. Loving Luca was also loving the child she had been.

"Did Papa David tell you that he and I were married in, how do you say the name of the town near here that starts with an 'R?'"

"Riquewihr?" His eyes brightened.

"Yes. In the tiny chapel."

"Madame Claire, it is a difficult word, but you are a fast learner, you can say it. *REE KA-veer.* Try."

"Ree...K—"

The doorbell rang. Remy was off like a shot, barking, his fur aquiver.

Gilbert stood. "Odd, no one ever visits on Noël." He fought a smile and headed for the door.

Luca grinned up at her.

Claire wondered what they were up to. Had they invited Sister Georgette?

"Joyeux Noël," came a voice.

Claire blinked. "Marti?" She jumped up and took Luca's hands. "Come meet my best friend!"

Arms open wide, Marti rushed into the salon. Shopping bags filled with beribboned gifts dangled from her wrists. Dragging suitcases, her husband, Stephen, followed in her wake.

"I was so worried when you didn't answer your phone." Tears flooded Claire as she embraced her dearest friend.

"You were on your way here!" Together, they laughed and cried and laughed again.

"We've spent the last twenty-six Christmases together; I couldn't let this one get away." Marti squeezed Claire. "Besides, it was the perfect excuse for Stephen to deliver on his promise of taking me to France."

Stephen pulled off his knit cap and scarf. "I owe it all to you, Claire." He collapsed into a chair. "Merci."

Gilbert introduced himself and Luca.

Luca took Marti's hand and gently kissed it. "I am enchanté to meet Madame Claire's dearest friend." He stared at Marti's husband. "But you look very sleepy Monsieur Stephen."

Marti bent down, like she was melting with love for the child, and hugged him. "I am enchanté to meet you, Luca."

Gilbert popped a Champagne cork, and Luca rushed to the bar for glasses, which Gilbert began filling. After Luca delivered a coupe to everyone, Gilbert splashed a tiny bit in Luca's coupe. Luca raised his. "Bien venue au Château Soltner."

Gilbert rested his hand on Luca's shoulder and raised his glass. "We are very happy to have you here, and we wish you a merry Christmas."

"Bien venue et joyeux Noël," Claire chimed.

"I am teaching Madame Claire French." Luca's dimples deepened. "She is a very fast learner."

"I suspect the travelers must be hungry?" Gilbert asked.

"Ravenous," replied Stephen.

"I will return in a moment."

Claire followed Gilbert into the kitchen. "You knew about Marti and Stephen and kept it a surprise."

"Bien sûr." He put his arms around her. "I hope you don't mind, but after you were so sad not to be sharing Christmas with Marti, I called her and invited them to stay with us."

"That was so very thoughtful and kind of you." She kissed him. He returned her affection with far more enthusiasm than she'd anticipated. Breathless, she eked out, "Merci."

The timer dinged. He let her go. "I must serve le déjeuner."

She wasn't finished. She waited for him to pull the quiche from the oven and set it down, then wrapped her arms around his waist. "Merci. Merci for inviting and welcoming my friends into your home."

"I hope you will consider this *your* home. You and I and Luca and Remy—we all welcome them together."

Claire smiled against tears, tears of happiness and joy.

"We'd like you to stay with us, but it looks like we might have to fight Marti for you." He smiled and picked up the quiche.

Her heart beat wildly. She'd been awake all night considering his job offer as vintner. He'd presented her with an entirely new career possibility, along with the adventure of living in France and being close to Luca and falling in love with Gilbert. Could she move here? She couldn't wait to discuss it with Marti. She picked up the plate of croissants and a pot of jam and followed him into the salon.

As they sipped and laughed and ate, Claire marveled at how her life had changed within a week. She felt warmer and more relaxed than she had over the past year, which had been chilled by an emptiness the loss of David had opened and couldn't be filled by the companionship of Marti and Stephen.

Luca clapped his hands. "I spy a large package, and I think it is time to open it, oui?"

"Oui," Claire replied. "It is a gift for you and Onc."

Luca wrapped his arms around the large box, lifted it, and placed it on Gilbert's lap. "Ready, Onc?"

"Let's do it," replied Gilbert.

Together they tore at the paper, opened the box, and pulled out the dog puppet. Gilbert took one set of the cross-sticks and Luca the other, and together they brought the dog to stand on his paws. Gilbert rotated his crosspiece, and Luca brought up one of the strings, which made the puppet tilt and dip his head.

Remy's fur trembled, and he woofed.

Claire laughed. Gilbert put out his hand to her. "Show us how to make him run."

Relieved the puppet man showed her how to operate the dog, she stood between them, tilting their hands, plucking the strings, wiggling the sticks.

Marti and Stephen snapped photo after photo, as Remy ran in circles and barked at his new competition.

Claire bent down and called Remy. He was at her side in a second. She hugged him and knew, for the first time in her life, that she'd fallen in love with a dog. She soaked in the warmth, the fun, the laughter, the love.

How could she ever leave this happy place?

Marti pulled out a package sporting hot pink and lime green polka dots. She held it out to Claire. "A surprise for you."

Claire accepted the box. "Your packages are in Seattle."

"We can wait. Open yours now."

Claire sat on the couch, and Luca sat next to her. "I can help," he offered as he ripped the wrapping paper.

The plain brown cardboard box gave no clues about the contents. She glanced at Marti, who studied the Christmas tree, refusing to give Claire any hint.

"A diamond necklace?" asked Luca. "A wide-screen TV?"

Claire laughed, removed the lid, and gasped. "My prototype!" She pulled out the swimsuit and held it up, showing it to Luca and Gilbert. "This is my invention." She turned to Marti. "How did you get this?"

Marti laughed. "I hounded Rick and guilted him into giving it to me." She crossed her legs and cupped her knee. "By the way, you owe him three-thousand dollars."

"What?"

"Kidding. He said to tell you, good luck because you'll need it."

Luca lifted the turquoise and green Spandex above his head. "This is your life-saving maillot?"

"Sadly, yes, Luca."

"Why are you sad?"

"Because it doesn't work."

He bit his lip, examining the floatation device, and then held it out to Gilbert. "Onc, you can fix this, right?"

Gilbert ran his fingers along the tubing. "This is like the Mae West Survival Vest?"

"Yes," exclaimed Claire. "You're familiar with the deign?"

"It saved thousands of lives in World War II, many of them Allied pilots and seamen and French sailors." He withdrew a metal cylinder. "But this is the wrong valve. And the cylinder is too big—it overinflated the tube, did it not?"

"Yes," echoed Claire and Marti.

He ran his fingers through his hair. "Luca, you think we might have the right size cylinder in the cave?"

Luca's face grew serious. His eyes pinched in concentration as he examined the metal cartridge. He ran his fingers through his hair as Gilbert had. "I think we do."

"Really? Why?" asked Claire.

"Onc is the winemaker. He is the engineer, and together, we figure out how to store and age the wine."

"So, you know how these cartridges work." Claire's heartbeat raced.

Luca gave a Gallic shrug, pushing out his bottom lip, lifting his little shoulders, his palms facing her. "It is a simple thing."

Claire suppressed a laugh.

Gilbert hugged his son. "And I know that you do not want the valve to release when it touches the water. You want the user to have control over activation, right?"

"Right!" Claire jumped up. "Yes! You both understand the concept!"

"It is not difficult." Luca looked a bit bored.

Gilbert held her invention tenderly, like a cluster of grapes. "We will work on this tomorrow for you."

"One problem. Do you know anyone thin enough to model this and test it?"

Luca stood, stuffed a ball of crinkled wrapping paper under his pajama top, thrust his arm up, and bent his wrist. His other hand rested at his waist, and he batted his eyelashes. "I will be your mannequin."

Their boisterous laughter drowned out the carols.

In her mind, Claire saw David, the day she'd met him at the café, striking the same pose, and hearing him exclaim, *Ah, you're here for the fashion!* A tear escaped, and she quickly wiped it away as she silently thanked David for his son.

Claire wrapped Luca in her arms and sat him on her lap and kissed him all over until he squirmed away to play with the dog puppet.

Gilbert smiled at her as he lifted his glass, silently toasting her. Raising her glass, she sighed with not only relief, but also, dared she trust her heart—love? She certainly admired Gilbert, and she loved the father he was to Luca.

Although she was excited about her invention finally working, really, did it matter? It certainly didn't make her as happy as loving Luca...and Gilbert.

Gilbert had seen her at her worst—as she grieved her husband, as she remembered being dragged from a river, as she slayed her monster of darkness. He said she was safe with him, and she felt safe and believed in and loved. What was winning a patent compared to being embraced by a loving family?

But selling a patent might pay for all the flights Marti and she would need to visit each other if she accepted Gilbert's offer.

Luca sat on the couch between Claire and Gilbert, smiling broadly. Was he up to something?

She clinked her glass to Luca's and reached over Luca to touch her glass to Gilbert's. After sipping, Gilbert leaned over Luca and whispered to her, "Je t'aime."

She whispered, "Je t'aime, aussi," and kissed him.

Luca giggled and clapped. "You are a very fast learner."

THE END

I hope you enjoyed *His Last Christmas Gift*. If so, you might like to try my award-winning series that takes place in France.

https://debraborchert.com/bonus/

Sister Georgette's
Fruit & Nut Holiday Cookies

You'll need a very large bowl and a stand mixer with a paddle or flat beater attachment. As a child, I made these aided only by a wooden spoon, but it is a huge and tiring job of mixing by hand. —Sister Georgette

Photo Courtesy shutterstock.com

Makes 5 dozen cookies

Ingredients

1 cup brown sugar

½ cup salted butter

2 eggs, beaten

½ cup buttermilk*

2 ½ cups flour

½ teaspoon baking soda

½ teaspoon salt

½ teaspoon cinnamon

½ teaspoon nutmeg

¼ teaspoon ground cloves

1 cup raisins

1 cup chopped dates

1 cup chopped walnuts

1 cup dried fruit** in any mixture you like

½ cup fresh cranberries finely chopped (If you can't find fresh, substitute dried)

½ cup brandy or 1 tablespoon of vanilla***

Directions

1. Mix dried fruits together and sprinkle the brandy or vanilla over the fruit, mix to moisten all the fruit, and allow to sit for an hour.

2. Sift dry ingredients together in a large bowl.

3. Cream butter until fluffy.

4. Add sugar. Continue to cream sugar with butter until fully incorporated.

5. Add beaten eggs and mix until fully incorporated.

6. Add dried fruit, with any of the brandy or vanilla left in the bowl. Mix well.

7. Add the fresh (or dried) cranberries and mix well.

8. Add nuts and mix well.

9. Mix the dough by alternating adding a ½ cup of the dried ingredients with a bit of the buttermilk and mix well after each addition. Dough will be sticky.

10. Preheat oven to 350 degrees. (350°F)

11. Use baking mats or a greased baking sheet.

12. Drop by a level tablespoonful onto the baking sheet. Allow room between the cookies as they spread a bit.

13. Bake for 10-15 minutes (the time varies due to the fruits you choose and whether you use brandy in the dough.)

14. The cookies will be done when they turn a golden brown and have tiny cracks on the top surface and look lumpy. If lightly touched, they will resist a bit, and if you insert a toothpick, it will come out clean.

15. Allow to rest on the baking sheet for 1–2 minutes.

16. Remove cookies from baking sheet and then place on a linen towel or a cooling rack.

17. Scrape any residue from the baking mats or sheet and grease the sheet again before adding fresh dough.

NOTES

*__Buttermilk__: If you don't have buttermilk, you can pour a teaspoon of white vinegar or lemon juice into a measuring cup and add enough milk to make a ½ cup. Set aside the mixture for ten minutes before adding it to the dough.

__Dried Fruits__: Suggested dried fruits: apples, apricots, blueberries, cherries, cranberries, currants, peaches, pears. **Dried citrus fruits, figs, mangoes, pineapple, plums and prunes will _NOT_ work in this recipe. (Candied fruits can be used, but they make the cookies very sweet.)

__Suggestion__: If you can find a Dried Mixed Berries Blend (8 ounces), a sweetened dried blend of cranberries, blueberries, cherries, and golden raisins, it works really well for this recipe, and I highly recommend it. I added ¼ cup chopped apricots and only ¾ cup raisins and the Mixed Berries Blend and dates to my cookies.

***__Optional Brandy__: If you don't want to use brandy (I use applejack), you can use a tablespoon of vanilla or maple syrup, but be sure to sprinkle whichever liquid you choose over the dried fruit, allow to sit for an hour, and add any remaining liquid to the mixture.

__Storage__: Use parchment paper or waxed paper to separate layers of cookies, as they will stick to each other, and place them in an airtight container. These cookies freeze well.

Taste Testers: If you make Sister Georgette's cookies and let me know your thoughts, I'll thank you in the Acknowledgement section of my next book. Send your comments to: debra@DebraBorchert.com

Thank you & Bon Appétit!

A Big Merci
to My Fabulous Taste Testers

Sister Georgette, also known as "The Author" has been working on her Holiday Fruit & Nut Cookies recipe for twenty-five years. She wishes to thank all the following bakers for their recommendations, additions, suggestions, and compliments.

Photo Courtesy Nancy J. Mastro

"An instant holiday tradition from the first bite. These were so popular that we had to make another batch. Perfectly sweet and satisfying in the most comforting way." —Tamatha Cain, author, *Song of the Chimney Sweep*

"Sister Georgette's Fruit & Nut Cookies were gobbled up during Thanksgiving! These were quite resourceful cookies. Since they're not overly sweet we had them with coffee at breakfast, snacks in between and an extra dessert alongside the pumpkin pie. What I loved was the inviting pop of the fresh cranberries next to gooey dried fruit. Please thank Sister Georgette for me!"—Joan Fernandez, author, *Saving Vincent*

"Festive and flavorful and have a rough and ready, home-made appearance. I intend to distribute them to selected neighbors and friends."—Carolyn Korsmeyer, author, *Riddle of Spirit and Bone* and *Making Sense of Taste: Food and Philosophy*

"Thanks for sharing this delicious recipe! My family really enjoyed these soft, cakey cookies. I found that Safeway's Signature Select Berries and Cherries blend worked very well with the dates and a mix of regular and golden raisins. My husband is a chocolate fiend, so I added a drizzle of chocolate ganache (dark chocolate melted with a splash of heavy cream) just to gild the lily."—Heather Martin, author, *Party Pieces*

"They were delicious! They have such a festive, holiday taste. They reminded me of the kind of cookies my Swedish grandmother used to make during the holidays. I think of her whenever I bite into one, which brings forth a very sweet memory."—Nancy Mastro, author *Solitary Walker*

"These cookies are absolutely delicious, indulgent and low in sugar. I used dried cranberries instead of fresh ones, and I added some maple syrup instead of brandy. These fruit and nut cookies bring together a symphony of flavors and textures that make them a sweet treat to warm up any mealtime!"—Tatyana Tweedie

Thanks to my exercise instructors, Michelle Stevens, MaryPat Reeves, and Mary Burton for allowing me to distribute Sister Georgette's cookies to my classmates and receive comments on the recipe. And the following exercisers: Maria Bartlow, Marie Cermark, Kathy Curnutt, Mary Ellen Ecok, Gyung, Cathy & Herb Hiegel, Mariga Horoszowski, Edris Kenan, Katie Kilbourne, Sheri Ogilvie, Mary Ann Rupe, and Betty Teel.

"Delicious." Kathy
"Tasty!" Cathy & Herb
"Outstanding." Mary Ellen
"Absolutely fabulous!" Liz
"Very good." Edris & Gyung
"They were delicious!" Michelle
"Just the right mix of fruits & nuts!" Katie
"I love fruit and nuts together. Brava." Betty
"Very tasty. I'm going to try to veganize it." Sheri
"The only way to get your fruit in. Excellent." Marie
"I made them for holiday guests. They were absolutely
fabulous." Liz

ten stories. I can't wait for the next one."—*The Good Life France*

"An engrossing depiction of feminine courage—a renegade heroine whose compassion for innocent people leads to both loss and love."—*Foreword's Book of The Day*

"An empowering and dramatic story of romance in deeply troubled times..."—*Self-Publishing Review*

"...fearless female lead. ...crafted by a master of relationships and emotional tension, making this revolutionary novel a tight, heart-pounding twister of a tale."—*The Independent Review of Books*

"Borchert's extensive research shines through a narrative that is enhanced by her mastery of character development. Borchert quickly immerses readers into the dangers of late 18th-century France and highlights the struggles of women seeking independence and equality."—*BookLife Editor's Pick*

"*Her Own War* is a stunning and fast-paced story that will keep you reading late into the night!"—Eliza Knight, *USA Today* and international bestselling author of *The Queen's Faithful Companion*

"Geneviève's courage, loyalty and independent spirit sparkle on every beautifully written and action-packed page ... a vibrant, enthralling story!"—Penny Haw, author of *The Woman at the Wheel* and *The Invincible Miss Cust*

"...the seamless blend of historical facts and fictional storytelling will keep you hooked until the very end. When historical fiction is crafted with such skill, there is no limit to its allure. The exceptional brilliance of this story will captivate you from start to finish and leave an indelible mark in your heart forever. Highly recommended." —*Coffee Pot Book Club*

"Filled with absorbing turns, this is a captivating story led by a courageous and likable heroine."—*Readers' Favorite 5 Star Review*

Page Turner Awards, Finalist: Book, Romance, and Book to Film Adaptation

Coffee Pot Gold Medal Winner Enlightenment (1600s-1800s)

Firebird Book Award Winner

Château de Verzat Series: Book Three

Chapter 1

Geneviève
Loire Valley, France
August 1797

Across the still Loire River dark clouds mushroomed above workers reaping hay. A rainstorm could harm the harvest; hail would ruin it.

Weeks of hot weather had ripened a bountiful grape crop, and all four hundred families who lived on the estate were in the vineyard furiously picking. I reached beneath the leaves, clipped grape clusters, and placed them in a large basket. Removing my straw bonnet, I wiped sweat from my brow and rubbed my lower back. Could this ache be a sign I was with child? There was no time to revel in the thread of hope running through me. Every harvested grape went toward paying taxes the estate owed.

A few feet away, Aurélia clipped a bunch of grapes and smiled at me, her round black eyes offering sympathy. Tall and slim, she moved with the grace of a poplar bending with a breeze. She pulled a fan from her hanging pocket and offered it.

"Thank you." I waved it, savoring the stirring air. A finely hand-painted scene on delicate silk depicted the Seine. "This is Paris. I hope when we are not at war, we can visit the city together." I closed it and held it out, but she put up her palm.

Wearing a simple blue day gown and long white apron, she had the regal bearing of a queen. She mouthed, *You need it more than I.*

I understood Aurélia, without her voice, although I hoped she'd regain her ability to speak. I tucked the fan into my belt and smiled at my past foolishness—I had feared I could never be friends with my former-lover's wife. Aurélia was more than a friend; she was the sister I had always wanted. "Were you able to speak before you were captured and enslaved?"

She grinned and brought her fingers to her thumb, repeatedly, indicating she never stopped talking.

"Do you miss your voice?"

She pretended to hold a baby in her arms and mouthed, *I miss singing.*

Down the hill, a distant spot of color caught my eye. Two officers on horseback trotted along the river road, their red frock coats flaring against the gray clouds.

The last officers conscripted four of our fine men, and they all died on the battlefield. I wiped my sticky hands on my apron. "I'll not let them take any more of our men to waste in their war." I searched the vineyard and spied my husband. "Louis!"

He stopped the team of horses pulling a wagon laden with grapes.

I pointed at the two soldiers.

He handed the reins to a worker and ran, shouting through the fields. Young men darted around vines. The officers would die of starvation before they found them in the network of Verzat caves.

The sky darkened. "Aurélia, a storm is coming. Best take the children to the château."

She mouthed, *Rain will be cooling.*

"But it might hail."

She shook her head. *We will be fine.*

I hoped she was right. My four-year-old stepdaughter sat on the dry, cracked earth holding a basket nearly as big as she was and waving her hand. "Tante Gen, why are there so many wasps?"

"They like the sweet juice." I swiped at a lock of hair stuck to my cheek. Louis and I had been married a year and still Louisa called me *aunt.* I feared I was not a good *maman,* but I didn't know how to be a better one.

Aurélia's three-year-old son sat on the ground next to Louisa, holding another basket. As she clipped clusters, Aurélia gently toyed with the vines, making the leaves tickle Charles. He threw back his head and laughed.

A low rumble stopped my picking. The advancing clouds darkened to the color of charcoal. "I pray the clouds empty themselves before they cross the river." The officers turned their horses and headed east, toward Tours. My shoulders relaxed as I resumed clipping. But a stirring in my stomach nagged me. Should I order everyone to seek shelter now in case of hail? The workers were so loyal, I doubted they would leave their work, but I could at least send the elderly and children inside.

Louisa screeched at a wasp. "I want to go home, now."

Lightning flickered over the distant hayfield. A louder rumble followed. Everyone continued their work. I dared not leave. I waved my apron over her. "I won't let them hurt you."

Charles reached out. "Take my hand, Louisa. I'm not afraid."

"You are very brave, Charles," I said.

Louisa grabbed his hand. "I'm brave, too."

Cold air dropped over us like a curtain. Lightning brightened the sky. Gooseflesh ran up my arms. A sharp odor, like scorched metal, sliced the air. Had lightning struck a wagon? Workers in the hayfield flung their scythes away and threw themselves flat upon the ground, covering their heads with their arms.

"Everyone!" I shouted, "Take shelter!"

The sound of a roaring river charged toward us.

Louisa screamed and covered her ears. I swept her up and brought her to my chest.

Lightning lashed across the sky like a whip. A deafening crash followed.

Torrents of rain poured down like we were standing under a waterfall. I bent over, protecting Louisa, and the force of water pushed the breath from me.

We dared not run for cover. Lightning sought the highest target, and that would be us, should we run.

The rain lessened. Pinging and clacking sounds seized my breath. "Hail," I shouted. "Aurélia. Cover Charles with your basket."

Pebbles of ice the size of pearls popped and bounced on the crusty earth.

"Papa!" Louisa cried. "I want Papa."

I grabbed her basket and dumped the grapes on the ground. Falling to my knees, I pushed Louisa down.

Aurélia slapped the ground under the vines.

"Good idea." I pulled Louisa under the vines for shelter. "Curl up on your side, like a puppy." She whined and fought me as I wrangled her under the basket. "Hush, you will be safe."

Aurélia brought Charles next to Louisa and put her basket over him. Louisa's fingers crept out from under the wicker and searched for Charles. His hand gripped hers.

Thunder boomed so loudly my teeth chattered. Hail needled my arms and face.

I screamed at the workers, "Cover your heads!"

With the children between us, Aurélia and I joined arms and pressed ourselves over the baskets. "Keep your head down and your bonnet covering your face."

Hail broke off chunks of my straw hat. Leaves and vines whirled past. Hailstones floated atop sheets of rainwater that slicked the impenetrable ground, pushing the pellets against the vine roots and piling up the hail like snowbanks. A shard of ice stung my cheek. I wiped the burn, and blood stained my fingers.

Louisa screeched and kicked the basket, knocking it off her. I lunged, pulled it atop her.

"I want Papa!" She kicked a hole in the basket, thrusting out her foot. I pushed it back.

Charles shouted, "Don't cry, Louisa. I'm here."

Ice chunks, now as large as plums, crashed over us like a rockslide.

Punishing hailstones pounded my back. A strange clacking noise surrounded us. Hailstones clattered atop piles of icy pellets. Blood dripped onto my skirts.

I prayed Louis and the pickers had taken cover under the wagon. Please, don't let it get worse. Please, let no one be injured. Please, don't destroy everything.

Lightning cracked. I counted to three before thunder boomed again. The storm was moving east of us—away from the vineyard, not deeper into it. I prayed the northern slope was spared. My grip on the basket eased. Please let everyone be safe.

The rumbling and crashing stopped as suddenly as it began. The wind calmed. Rain pattered. Ceased. Hailstones bobbed in rainwater, mixed with the dust, and sluiced around us in chalky streams. A bank of ice surrounded my legs, making me shiver.

Strong sunlight beat upon my back. I straightened, squinting in the brilliant light. Where was Louis?

Broken shoots dangled from vines. Splintered canes stabbed the earth. Battered leaves and smashed grape clusters littered the vineyard. A blackbird lay squawking, fluttering its crippled wing.

We were ruined.

ACKNOWLEDGEMENTS

A Huge Thank You To

Dr. Berry Edwards who often resorted to speaking French to drag me back from France while writing. Thank you for making me laugh. You are my chevalier.

Aunt Di for your love, support, laughter, and being crazy with me.

Holly Williams for her friendship and expert knowledge of the French language. Any mistakes are my own.

My Great Aunt Margaret who dazzled me with her creativity and taught me to hand-sew Christmas ornaments.

Dr. Reese Abright who thought the life-saving device was disguised as a bust-enhancer. Thank you for allowing me to employ that brilliant idea.

Critique partners, first readers, and editors who asked the right questions and demonstrated great insight, patience, humor, and honesty: Jann Alexander, Tiffanny Brooks, Joan Fernandez, Joanne Khuns, Jill MacGregor, Nancy J. Mastro, Lorin Oberweger, Linda Rosen, Jane Sutherland, Terri Thayer, Jennifer White.

My fellow supportive writers of the Historical Fiction Affinity Group of Women's Fiction Writers Association: You all ROCK!

Librarians everywhere. You are my heroes.

Communities in which I have participated with many generous writers: Free Expressions, Historical Novel Society, Romantic Novelists' Association, The History Quill, Women's Fiction Writers Association.

Christina Consolé for including my books in her Parisian Page Turners. If you're looking for a book club that reads and discusses books that take place in France, check out her Parisian Page Turners: www.parisianniche .com/parisian-page-turners

A Special Thank You to Patrick Simmons and His Team at the Bellevue Aquatic Center

In researching drowning and water safety, I consulted Patrick Simmons. I've worked out at the Bellevue Aquatic Center for more than twenty-five years, at which Patrick is the Aquatics Program Manager of an awesome team of lifeguards, teachers, coaches, and staff. Every member of his team is affable, professional, helpful, and cheerful. Thank you, Patrick, for explaining the intricacies of water safety and to all your team members for helping me stay fit and sane while I write fiction in my head as I work out.

About Sitosterolemia

When I was writing this book, I read an article by Joe M. Moore in *The Wall Street Journal* (November 23, 2024) [https://www.wsj.com/health/healthcare/i-was-in-great-health-so-why-were-my-arteries-clogged-3a918640] in which he described his diagnosis of a rare heart condition. Joe was in great health but shocked to learn the results of a test that revealed blockages in three of his arteries exceeding 90 percent. In his article he described his journey of diagnosis.

Sitosterolemia is a symptomless, rare condition in which the body absorbs an excessive amount of plant sterols. The condition can be passed to a child from one parent or both parents and can affect people as early as childhood. Untreated, it can lead to premature coronary artery disease and death. With a timely and proper diagnosis, it can be treated with diet and drugs.

Joe wrote the article to increase the awareness of Sitosterolemia for both patients and medical professionals. He's writing a memoir, "The Excavation: Uncovering God's Hand in an Authentic American Life."

For more information, please visit:

American Heart Association

https://www.ahajournals.org/doi/10.1161/circ.150.suppl_1.4112869

Boston Children's Hospital

https://www.childrenshospital.org/conditions/
sitosterolemia

National Library of Medicine

https://www.ncbi.nlm.nih.gov/books/NBK572142/

National Organization for Rare Disorders

https://rarediseases.org/rare-diseases/sitosterolemia/

About the Author

This photo is a Polaroid outtake from a photoshoot in the early 1980s, during which time I worked as a model and actress to pay for my tuition at the Fashion Institute of Technology.

Photo Courtesy Macy's Herald Square Studio

Macy's hired me to advertise Totes umbrellas. In the ad I am wearing the same costume worn by the famous Santa of the Macy's Thanksgiving Day Parade in New York City—which celebrates its 100-year anniversary in 2026.

Most people think modeling and acting are glamorous jobs, but I found this career to be arduous, although fun and lucrative work. For the Totes advertisement I wore the gargantuan Santa coat of thick red wool trimmed in white fur. Hand-tooled leather cuffs and suspenders with hand-painted white edelweiss flowers and red holly berries, trimmed with large brass jingle bells were added. The coat weighed about ten pounds and was terribly warm—especially under hot lights. I also wore Santa's hat which was clipped in the back with clothespins to fit my head. The photographer directed me to angle the Totes umbrella over my head for more than an hour. To this day I can remember trying not to sweat and my arms aching for three days.

The stylist and photographer were delightful to work with. We shot in the department store's studio which was located on the top floor of Macy's Herald Square store. For appearing in this ad, I was paid $100 an hour and worked for two hours, earning a total of $200, less my agency's 20% commission, $160—which would be $625 today.

When I lived in New York City, my studio apartment was a block from Columbus Circle and every Thanksgiving I hung out my window, straining to the right, to watch the parade march down Broadway. Macy's Santa suit looked much better on the man they hired to portray jolly old Saint Nick. I was younger then, but I am just as enthusiastic about Christmas.

May all your holidays be merry and bright.

Spreading the Word

Word of mouth is the best way to discover books, so if you'd like to help spread the word, please share your review. Your feedback is greatly appreciated, and your review will help film producers discover the potential movie within this book.

If you'd like a complimentary e-story or a recipe, visit:

Do you enjoy images of Christmas around the world? If so, visit my Pinterest page for photos I've taken in Paris and Alsace.

https://www.pinterest.com/debraborchert/christmas-in-alsace-france/